Crumbling Deception

A Culinary Cozy Mystery

Alice Stone

MM Innovative Creations

Contents

19. Chapter 19

Chapter 1

Chapter 1

My life was great. Until my landlord decided to be the victim of the first homicide in Hillgrove since 1998.

"I swear I didn't kill Marco."

My outburst takes the female detective by surprise. She is quite young as compared to the composed man beside her. His light-colored eyes are a stark contrast against his inky black hair. I would've appreciated them better if they weren't currently drilling holes into my forehead straight into my brain. It isn't hard to decipher that these two detectives have been put together in the classic good cop, bad cop routine. *With her blonde hair and empathetic wide eyes, she is the sunny to his shady.*

When she shakes her head, ready to calm me down, he places his crossed arms on the metal table—reminding me of the uncomfortable metal chair painfully flattening my butt—and leans forward.

"We never said you did."

His condescending tone strikes a chord, and I find myself snapping at a homicide detective.

"I sensed the implication."

He narrows his drilling machines to slits. Sensing the rising tension, the good cop intervenes.

"Miss Grayson, we just need you to recap your side of the story."

Turning away from the infuriating detective, I take a deep breath and nod. The sooner I tell them what they want to hear, the sooner I can leave. The closet-sized interrogation room is no place for me. I have a business to run.

"Okay."

Approximately twenty-four hours ago...

The alarm on my bedside table rings at six a.m. sharp. I drop my shoe to turn it off before it wakes Loki, my lovingly annoying cat. All dressed for my morning run, I jog down the street. Like clockwork, Polly is already out in her garden with a large travel mug in hand. I wave at my next-door neighbor and she returns it with a big smile.

My usual track takes me on a thirty-minute run through our neighborhood and into the forest, where I sometimes sit by the stream for a while, before running back home. The loud chirping of birds complimented by the rush of the flowing stream, really kickstarts my day to a great start. Living in Paris for a couple of years, I'd learned to appreciate nature more. It's a loss for everyone here who doesn't.

Each run enforces what I already knew; moving to Hillgrove was the right decision. It is peaceful, naturally loud, and has a tight knit community. After living amidst the bustling crowd of huge cities for nearly ten years, Hillgrove's quaint little town was a calling I couldn't ignore anymore.

Once I'm back home, I take a quick shower and get ready for the day. I am more on the leaner side. I grew up taller than most of my class in school. It often made me the butt of the joke before Charlie—star athlete then, my ex-husband now—and I started dating.

I put on a solid mauve set and heels. Loki climbs up on the dressing table and shapes himself into a perfect loaf, watching me as I try to tame my wild, wavy brown locks in a fancy twist. Leaving him a few kisses to last him a day, I fill his food bowl and gather my own supplies into my tote bag before walking out to the shed to grab my bicycle.

"Lily!"

I stop pedaling in front of Polly's lawn. She walks towards me, waving a phone charger in hand. I open my bag and sure enough, my charger is missing. Coming to a stop beside me, she drops it inside.

"You forgot it next to the coffee table."

Right. I had dinner at her place last night and almost fell asleep there because of how tired I was.

I smile at her, "Thanks."

"Bring me a cupcake, you know which one," she winks, adjusting my hair over my shoulder.

Of course I know which one. I know everyone's favorite by now. My café bakery, Cups & Cakes, is on the commercial side of town. I was lucky enough to snag a good deal. The shop had just been vacated by a retiring baker. People in Hillgrove are loyal, even to a spot they bought their bread from. So when I started my business and offered good deals on more baked goods; cupcakes, muffins, cookies, bread etc., they flocked to my shop like pigeons.

I unlock the back door to my shop that leads into the kitchen, then park my bike and pick up my belongings. My eyes stray to the other locked door in the alley. It also leads into a kitchen. In fact, the door opens into my shop's architectural twin. With one wall connecting them, they both open into main streets. I know this because I've dreamt of owning it ever since I bought this one.

Marco might have given up on my abilities but I haven't and never will. I will pay him the rent that is due and I'll also buy the other shop from him. *He'll see.*

Switching on the lights, I take in the place for a second. This spot right here is the place where everything seems easy. I tie my apron and put on my hair cap. Every task just flows after that, more muscle memory than thought. Tray after tray goes into the ovens.

I'm on my last cupcake batch for the day when the back door opens. I startle at the interruption and the plastic cone drops from my hand, splattering batter around it.

Max winces at the mess, "My bad."

I mockingly glare at my friend and coworker. We met while interning at a restaurant in Paris. I learned many years ago that staying mad at him for too long is impossible. His Ken-like appearance gets him out of many, if not all, tight spots.

"You're early."

"Actually, I'm right on time."

"Let me rephrase," I hold up a finger. "You're early by *your* standards."

He smiles, his brilliant teeth sparkling, "I was woken up by a bird slamming into my window. Got up to check if it was okay and couldn't go back to sleep."

"So I have a bird to thank for your rare punctuality?"

He nods, his shiny brown hair flopping on his forehead.

"Alright pretty boy, grab your apron. You can complete the last batch. I'll go open up the front."

Leaving the apron and hair cap in the kitchen, I make a quick pit stop in my office. The pale pink walls that I painted myself are the only thing that give this room a personality. I still haven't gotten around to remodeling, and it has already been two years.

Nevertheless, the show must go on.

I plug my phone in to charge and leave the office. At the front, I switch on the dimmer lights for the day, lift the blinds, wipe the tables and countertops, and flip the sign on the door to 'open'. Then go grab fresh batches of baked goods. The shop slowly fills with my favorite aroma.

The coffee makers are filled and ready-to-go cups lined up for early customers, when Rhea enters the shop at 7:45 a.m. on the dot. Her five-year-old son, zooms in behind her, way too energetic for eight in the morning. She is one of my first customers every day. Marco would come in soon too.

Needing her morning fix of caffeine, it is a bonus that she also gets my low sugar cookies for her diabetic son. Did I develop the recipe especially for him? Yes. Did I use it to gain more customers? Definitely yes.

"Jay watch your step," Rhea cautions him as she approaches the counter.

"Hi Jay!" he waves at me before being distracted by the display. "Good morning, Rhea."

"Is it?" she deadpans.

I notice the prominent bags under her eyes that weren't there a week ago.

"Are you okay?"

Her face falls. She sighs while taking out her wallet, "My husband got fired from his job last week. So I've been taking double shifts."

I pick up a paper bag and, deep in thought, slowly pack her order of three sugar-free chocolate chip cookies, two blueberry muffins, and a large cup of coffee. When she puts down fifty dollars on my counter, I slide them back to her along with her order.

"Today is on the house." I smile at her cheerfully, "Enjoy!"

Her smile lights up her eyes, tiredness melting away for a moment.

"Oh Lily! I can't thank you enough. You don't know how much I needed that."

Actually, I *do* know. Before I can reply, Max comes out with a fresh batch of strawberry cupcakes. I turn to look at Rhea, always amused by the 'Max effect', as I like to call it in my head.

"Hey Mrs. G—"

Rhea immediately cuts him off, blushing as red as her hair, which she twirls with her free hand.

"Oh Max, I've told you a million times. Just call me Rhea."

Max moves to stand beside me, running a manicured hand (though he would never admit getting a manicure. But being a woman, I know a manicure when I see one) through his perfect hair.

"Sure." He nods, smiling at her. "Would you like something else?"

Right before she drools, her son tugs at her shirt.

"Mama, let's go. Mama!"

She tuts, "Okay fine, let go of my clothes!"

Then she turns to us with a smile. "Thank you, Lily, *Max*," she practically sighs his name and leaves.

I stifle a giggle, but Max elbows it out of me.

"Shut up, it's not funny," he groans.

I laugh, "I didn't say anything."

"You're laughing."

"Yeah, because you're pretty and you work out too, which is uncommon here, so you're bound to gain attention from the women, or men, of Hillgrove. I don't know why you get so defensive."

Before I even finish speaking, I know my words will rub him the wrong way, and he'll get even more defensive. Which is why it takes me by surprise when he steps forward towards me.

"Because they're not the one I want attention from."

With his unwavering blue eyes holding me in place, it isn't hard to decipher what he means. But I play it off, like I always do.

"Do you smell that? I think something's burning."

With that, I rush off into the kitchen, telling him to man the front. I sigh in relief when he doesn't follow. He is my friend. I don't have many, to begin in the first place. I would very much like to keep him as my friend than risk it for something that wouldn't last.

I stay in the kitchen for the next eighty minutes. With nothing else to do, I bake a new recipe of almond bread. I'm waiting for the oven's buzzer when Max shows up.

"You gave away a free order again?"

I shut my eyes and sigh. *Not this again.*

"Lily, you can't keep giving away big orders. A cupcake is fine. But a whole order? You lost thirty-six dollars at the start of a business day."

"She'll come back in a week and buy three whole batches for her son's birthday. It was a calculated risk, Max," I try to appease him.

"What if she's too broke to do so? What then?" He throws his arms out when I don't answer. "I need a minute."

He leaves through the back door. Righteous anger heats my blood. The kitchen door slams behind me as I storm to the front. I hate it when he tells me how to run my business. I didn't tell him to follow me here to Hillgrove. He did it on his own. If I had wanted a partner, I would've asked.

Starting their work days, people pour in to get their coffees and quick snacks. I put on a smile for them and make small talk while giving them what they need. A couple of people put their change into the tip jar. Thirty minutes later, Max returns with a sheepish look on his face. He lifts up a hand to reveal a paper bag.

"I got you brunch."

At the sight of Tina's logo, and undoubtedly the meat lover's sandwich inside, I grab it from him and pull out my bar stool from beneath the shelf. One of the things I love most about running Cups & Cakes in Hillgrove is that no one cares if I eat behind the counter. Our customers are enjoying their food, why shouldn't I? Max takes his spot behind the counter while I eat. Just like that, our disagreement is easily forgotten.

While I'm eating, a thought occurs to me.

"Hey Max, did Marco show up while I was in the kitchen?"

He shakes his head, still counting the coins, "No. He didn't come in today."

I frown, "That's strange."

"Maybe he'll come before closing?"

I barely form another word, interrupted by a loud crash at the door. Flustered customers all look at the source and I follow their gazes to see Cora standing in the doorway, a broken plant pot at her feet, dirt spread all over my floor.

As I shoot to my feet, Max stops me.

"I'll handle it. Please stay here."

I do as he says, but glare at Cora, who just smirks making it very clear that this wasn't an accident. Max has a talk with her and she leaves without causing another scene like she usually does. One would think that my ex-husband's twin would show me some decency. But no. She is still the devil she was when we were in high school. Having her flower shop right next to me is the only thing I hate about this location.

"She said she slipped," Max says, grabbing the broom from the supply closet.

I scoff, "Of course, she did."

Four hours later, around two p.m., I see people going for their lunch breaks across the street. Soon, when I expand my business and buy the shop behind me, I'll see people heading towards my restaurant too.

I daydream, while wrapping up the leftover muffins for old Mr. Williams. He is the bookstore owner in this lane. I remember going to his bookstore every day of each summer when I was younger. I was surprised to see that he still works at the bookstore when I returned to Hillgrove.

Max returns from his break. I pick up Mr. Williams's tea and muffins.

"I'll be at the bookstore."

I turn back around when he doesn't reply.

"Max?"

He looks up from his phone then. "Yeah sure."

I shake my head, smiling. As soon as I hit the road, a weird sense of unease hits me. People stand crowded in corners of streets, whispering to each other. Their eyes stray to each other but no one waves or smiles like they commonly do.

The bell dings on the door as I enter the bookstore. Mr. Williams, noticing my confusion, ushers me in and closes the blinds. The wrinkles on his face are deepened by his frown.

"Mr. Williams, what's going on?"

"Marco is dead."

Chapter 2

Chapter 2

"So you're saying that you didn't see him yesterday?" The kind detective confirms.

I nod, "Yes."

"And your coworker, Max Sloan," she confirms his name from her notepad, "could he have served him while you were unavailable?"

"He didn't. Marco didn't come to the shop yesterday."

"His wife says he left for work on time. Everyone knows his first stop is your shop."

I blink at the other detective when he finishes speaking, trying to figure out the best way to answer his *question*. When he doesn't elaborate, my tongue works of its own accord.

"Is there a question in there?"

His mouth turns down. In response, mine turns up. Blondie jumps in.

"Lily— may I call you Lily?" I nod at her, and she continues. "I know this is most unpleasant. But you have to understand that we have a job to do. This ordeal is going to blow up in town due to obvious reasons. And I'm sure it will not be bringing any good fame towards your business."

My shoulders hunch at her words. "I'm sorry. I just don't want to be here. But that doesn't mean that I want to cause any problems."

"That's okay. We have no more questions for now."

"Don't skip town," the male detective adds.

"Wasn't planning on it."

I quickly leave the suffocating room and keep my head down, watching my skirt swish between my legs as I walk out of the precinct. A heavy feeling settles in my gut. Marco is dead. *Killed.* There's a killer in our small town. With a population of less than a thousand, this is supposed to be the safest place in the country. I startle at the sound of my phone ringing in my pocket. Taking it out, I stop and rest against a wall.

"Hi Mom."

"Lily? How are you faring? Where are you? Please tell me you're not alone."

"Slow down, momma. I'm near the community center. Just left the precinct."

"What? Why?"

"They called me this in morning. Just a simple procedure," I quickly explain when she gasps, "Nothing to worry about."

"Lily Eva," I wince as she middle-names me. "I'll worry about whatever I want to. You come home this instant."

"Mom I can't just—"

I stare at the screen as the tone beeps, signaling the end of the call. *Great.* She hung up on me. I go to my bakery first, since I am a rational woman who thinks with her head.

Max looks up as soon as I enter through the front. He was interviewed earlier and covered here while I went for mine. He covers the distance in two long strides and bends down to wrap me in a hug. It's not that I'm short, I'm a good five-eight. But he's just really tall. And his hugs are very comforting. We stay like that for a while before I realize that we're not alone and have a couple of people in the shop.

I step back and clear my throat, scratching at my forehead to re-member what I was supposed to say to him.

"Are you okay?" he asks, his hands holding my shoulders.

"Yes." I answer automatically, before it hits me that it's okay to not be okay today. "No. Not really."

"Me too."

"I think we should close the shop for the day. I definitely need some time with my family."

"You can go. I'll lock up."

"You sure?"

He just smiles and nudges me towards the back. I get my bag and lock my office, leaving through the back where my bicycle is. My family lives in the neighborhood behind the commercial zone. It's where I grew up. Now it's where my brother's growing up. Yes, I have a twenty years younger adopted brother.

My parents are both retired doctors. My mother was a pediatrician and my father was a surgeon. Luke was admitted as a small toddler. He suffered an accident at the orphanage in a nearby town that caused him to lose parts of his tongue. My parents, who were both his doctors, developed a strong connection to him, and four months later, they adopted him. When he was little, we all learned ASL. My parents taught him as he grew. Because by then I had gotten married and had left Hillgrove. I will always regret not being around to witness him growing up. But that's just life, prioritizing the wrong things at the wrong times.

I stop as I see an alleyway cordoned off with yellow tape. Police cars are parked in front of it to stop onlookers like me from getting too close. Yet, people are still gathered near the street. I get off my bike and drag it with me towards the alley. There's hardly anything to be seen. I bet they're just gathering fingerprints or other evidence now.

Murmurs reach my ears.

They're saying he was poisoned...

Who would do such a thing?

He gets coffee from Cups & Cakes...

I approach the huddle.

"Hello there."

They all jump, surprised by the intrusion. Their eyes flit from side to side, looking everywhere but straight at me.

"I'm not Medusa, you know?"

My attempt at a joke falls flat as the group doesn't smile, let alone laugh. I turn to Rhea's husband.

"How's the job search going, Tom?"

The tips of his ears turn red as he looks at the ground for an answer. His aunt, who is a member of the town council, glares at me. I realize he must not have mentioned his joblessness to his present company. My own cheeks heat up.

"Umm... good luck with it. Have a good day y'all."

Y'all? Seriously? I cringe mentally. This whole murder thing is really throwing me off. I don't look back as I cycle away. Reaching my parents' home in record time, I lay down my bike next to the swing set in the lawn and walk to the backyard. Sure enough, I find my dad tinkering away at his old car. His habit of fixing humans turned into fixing cars after his retirement.

"Pop!"

My attempt to scare him works when he bumps his head on the open door as he looks up. Seeing it's me, he jumps to his feet, opening his arms for me. I rush to safety and smile as he sways us back and forth.

"How you holdin' up, muffin?"

"I'm good, Dad."

He puts enough distance between us to look at me clearly. His bushy eyebrows draw close behind his wire-rimmed spectacles. I ruffle his grey-streaked chestnut hair.

"I really am."

"Okay off you go then, Luke is waiting to hear all about it."

I draw back in surprise, "He knows?"

Dad just raises an eyebrow. I sigh.

"Of course, he knows. This is Hillgrove."

He laughs, "And don't you just love it?"

I roll my eyes but laugh too. A clap gains my attention and I turn to see Luke standing at the stairs. I swear he's taller than he was the previous week when I saw him last. I wave at him and he signs in reply.

'Come inside and have lunch with me.'

I laugh at his bossiness and offer him a salute. "Sir, yes sir!"

He just rolls his round, brown eyes and walks inside. I excuse myself from Dad and follow the young guy. Mom's kitchen smells distinctly of herbs and cheese.

I nudge Luke, "Lasagna?"

He nods with a huge grin on his face. My stomach grumbles in response. Mom appears out of thin air with two loaded plates in her hand. I kiss her cheek as she sets them in front of us on the dinner table.

"Thank you."

She pats my cheek, "You've lost weight. Eat up."

With that, she is gone again. I stuff a spoonful into my mouth. Luke clears his throat. I turn to him. He signs, *'So?'*

"So what?"

He rolls his eyes again and I flick him on the forehead. He winces and rubs the spot while glaring at me.

"They'll get stuck like that if you keep rolling them. Plus, you're not supposed to be this sassy until you're eighteen."

'You got a tattoo when you were fifteen.'

"And it got infected," I fib straight through my teeth while stuffing my face. "Dad had to cut it out of my skin."

His eyes widen and he goes a little green in the face.

"Now," I change the topic before he throws up near my lasagna, "I'll tell you what's going on, but only after we finish eating."

We eat in silence for a moment when, as expected, he caves. I look at him as he signs.

'Did you really poison Marco?'

My food goes down the wrong pipe, and I choke, coughing to get some air in. He calmly pats my back and hands me a glass of water, like he didn't just ask me if I murdered a man. As soon as I can speak, I turn to him.

"Obviously not Luke! Do you think I'm capable of doing that?"

'You did hit Cora with your car once.'

I throw my hands up, "Okay first of all, where are you getting your information from? Secondly, she cut a hole in my running shorts that day. I spent the whole gym class running around with my butt on display! So yes, I *nudged* her with my car. She didn't even stumble. And lastly, I am not a murderer, you psycho."

'I was just making sure.'

I make a face at him and resume eating. A few seconds later, I drop my fork.

"Did someone say something to you?"

'About what?'

"You know..." I shrug, "About me being responsible."

'No, I was just messing with you.'

He deflects my hand and saves himself from a smack to the head, instead he maneuvers into reach and tugs at my braid.

"Ow!"

"No fighting at the table!" Mom yells from somewhere in the house.

"Jerk," I mutter underneath my breath.

He signs a not so-very-kind word at me. I pretend not to have seen it.

*****

After a whole evening of cleaning, playing charades, and watching senseless television, I stand up and stretch. Mom's phone dings just as I do.

"I think I should head back now."

With Dad half-asleep, Luke already passed out, and Mom on her phone, no one answers me.

"Mom, I'm leaving."

She shakes her head, her expression somber as she looks at me, "Oh Lils, I don't think you should."

"Why?" I ask her, immediately on guard. "What's wrong?"

She hands me her phone. I see that it's a group chat at the hospital. Apparently, she is still a part of it. I open the latest document and see that it is an autopsy report. When I realize whose, my knees tremble and I have to sit. Mom puts an arm around my shoulders and takes the phone from my hands.

"I know you respected him a great deal. You don't owe anyone any answers."

"Mom," my voice shakes as I speak, "what does it say?"

She takes a deep breath and when she speaks, it's in her doctor voice.

"He was poisoned. It took approximately an hour for the symptoms to occur, which means he was poisoned between eight to nine a.m."

I shudder, only to freeze in place when my phone rings. Mom hands it to me and I almost don't want to pick it up when I see who is calling.

"Well," Mom says, looking at my screen, "you don't owe anyone answers, *except the police.*"

Chapter 3

Chapter 3

"Do you know why you're here again?"

Detective Roberts; straight to the point like always. That's right. This time I memorized his name. I force a grin on my face.

"Maybe because you missed me?"

I can hear the indifference in his voice as he continues speaking, "It's because you conveniently left out a huge detail earlier."

"I don't think so."

I mentally tell myself to stop fidgeting with the clasp of my bracelet. But it's no use. If I don't fidget, they'll see my hands shaking. I'm sure shaking is a bigger tell for nervousness than fidgeting.

"So, you're saying you didn't have an argument with Marco Sanchez the day before he died?"

My bracelet slips from my wrist onto the ground. I look down at it, lamenting the fact that I'll have to wait till the end to pick it up.

I finally look up at him. I don't know if he looks different because it is late or if it's due to the light stubble on his face. But I do want to know what color his eyes are. They are striking.

"He yelled. I listened. Would hardly call that an argument."

"Sure." With one nod and a word he has perfectly made it clear that he doesn't believe me. "Why did he yell?"

"Because I am behind on my payments."

Detective Williams frowns, "Isn't *Cups & Cakes* doing well?"

I smile at her, "It is. I want to buy another shop and have a— *had* a deal with Marco. But saving money is a time-taking process, and sometimes he thought letting me know, *in a loud voice*, that I'm a bad investment was a good way to speed things up. It wasn't the first time, and it wouldn't have been the last."

"Did you have a tumultuous relationship with Mr. Sanchez?" She asks.

I shake my head. "He gave me a chance to start anew. I owe him. He might have yelled at me at times, but he had a soft heart. He always came back the next day. Which is why I noticed when he *didn't*."

My voice breaks on the last word and I stop talking, gulping down the sudden lump in my throat.

"On the day he died," she finishes for me.

I nod, unable to speak at the moment. The last thing I want to do is cry in front of them.

"That's enough for today. You can leave."

Detective Williams looks surprised by Detective Roberts letting me off the hook, but she doesn't contest him. Nor do I. The chair screeches on the floor as I stand up too fast. I stop it before it can make more of that awful sound, apologize, and get the hell out of there.

"Dear god," I huff and take a fresh breath of air outside the precinct, blinking to get rid of the pesky tears. *Who knew police stations were that suffocating?*

I'm surprised to see Dad still waiting for me in his truck. Out of the blue, it occurs to me that Stella was right when she said that because I spent all my twenties fending for myself—even when I was married—I now have trouble believing that someone would be there for me without an ulterior motive. Stella, my best and oldest friend, who'll have a field day when I admit it to her.

I walk up to Dad's window instead of getting in. He rolls it down when he sees me.

"All clear?" he asks.

I nod.

"I'll drop you home."

I shake my head.

"Words please," he politely urges.

"I love you, Dad."

His smile widens, creasing his eyes. "I love you too, Lils."

"Now go home," I say before walking to the back to take out my bicycle.

"Drop a text—"

"When I reach home," I finish for him. "You too."

***

I sign off on the chart and hand it back to the delivery boy. He's a teenager who looks like he wishes to be anywhere but here. I tell myself that has nothing to do with why I tip him big and the only reason is that I'm generally a good tipper. It almost, *almost,* redeems me in his eyes and he offers me the tiniest of smiles before gunning it. I sigh as I take the handles of the trolley, holding a week's worth supply of eggs, and start pushing it towards the alley.

Out of nowhere, someone slams into me, causing me to lose my footing. Whoever it is, grabs onto my clothes. Reflexively, I tighten my hold on the trolley, which topples under the weight of two people. Trays from the top two shelves tumble off and splatter on the ground beside and on me before I push the trolley upright. Covered in eggs, with a bruised bank balance and ego, I turn around to see who it is. The witchy curls of blonde hair immediately light me up on fire.

"What the hell Cora?!" I shove her away from me and stand up even as my legs tremble from the rush of adrenaline.

Unperturbed by the egg yolk dripping from her hair, she just sits there.

"A sorry would suffice," she snaps.

"*Sorry?*" I scoff. "Did you hurt your head on the way up to Earth from hell?"

"Excuse me?" her voice grates on my ears like nails on a chalkboard.

"Need I remind you that *you* bumped into me."

"Why on earth would I want to be anywhere near a poisonous schemer like you?"

As soon as she utters those words, they echo inside my mind until everything falls into place. I gasp as it dawns on me.

I point a finger at her, "It was you!"

Her face loses all color and she suddenly goes whiter than a ghost. "What the hell are you talking about?"

"It was you who told the police that Marco argued with me! It was you who spread rumors about me around town. And now everyone is terrified of me because of you!"

To my surprise, she smirks and looks around pointedly. "Oh no honey, that's all you."

I follow her gaze and my anger evaporates, doused by a cold awareness that pours over me as I see people crowded in the street, watching us with horrified wide eyes. No—watching *me* with horrified wide eyes. I suddenly realize how it looks to them; her on the ground with me standing over and shouting at her.

I am shocked when she yells in a loud voice all of a sudden.

"I said I'm sorry! What else do you want from me?"

Just then a tall shadow falls between us before she can advance with playing the victim. I look up at Max. He takes a second to gauge the situation and immediately acts accordingly. Putting a firm hand under her arm, he lifts Cora to her feet. She doesn't say anything to him. Not with her magnificent crush on him obstructing her senses. Once she is dealt with, he turns to me. I fist my burning palms as his eyes skim over me.

"Come on," he motions over his shoulder and starts pulling the trolley.

With one last look at the familiar faces in the street, I pick up the empty trays from the ground and throw them in the dumpster in the alley. I wait for Max to push the trolley up the slope and into storage before I close the door behind us. The sink starts to smell like eggs as I wash up my arms. My palms sting too, though not as much as my heart.

It is unbelievable how quickly everyone in town has turned suspicious of me, when I have spent the past two years doing nothing but gaining a good standing in the community.

"Come here."

I put a mental lid on the disappointment and face Max. He approaches me with a washcloth in hand. I don't know why I flinch when he raises it up to my face.

He chuckles, "Relax, I'm just trying to fix you up. You look like a dirty kitten. Smell like one too," he adds, bunching up his nose.

My neck and shoulders remain tense as he cleans my hair. When he backs up, I breathe, only to recoil again when he comes back with a clean, wet one. I take it from his hand.

"I can do it. Thank you."

He sighs and steps away, running his hands through his hair.

"What the hell just happened Lily?"

I stop short at his words and tone. "What do you mean?"

"I mean outside with Cora."

"She made me fall on purpose!" my own voice rises in sharpness.

Max pinches the bridge of his nose, before he lowers his hand and looks at me with clear judgement in his eyes.

"She wanted to make a scene. And she succeeded. Why can't you just try to pretend to be perfect until everyone calms down?"

I am rendered utterly shocked. My mouth opens and shuts twice, unable to form words. He rubs a hand over his face.

"I didn't mean it that—"

"I'm going to head home and shower. Can't be perfect smelling like eggs, can I?"

I ignore his murmurs of trying to stop me and leave.

As soon as I enter home, Loki comes running. He must have sensed that I'm not having a good day because he doesn't usually greet me like this.

"Hi there," I bend down to rub his head, and am immediately overwhelmed by the smell as my hair falls around me.

I laugh as Loki takes one sniff and then races down the hall, away from me.

"Nice to know you love me unconditionally, bud," I call out after him.

He meows in response from the bedroom.

***

Mr. Williams hands me a steaming cup of tea. Freshly showered, scrubbed, and having had a cry-fest, I realized I needed to talk to someone, other than Loki. Since Stella has picked the worst time possible to take a vacation, Mr. Williams seemed like the best option.

His cotton-white hair is combed neatly into a side part. I've never seen him in rumpled clothing in all the time I've known him. He is always sharply dressed.

"Thank you, Mr. Williams. I can't tell you what a relief it is that you haven't turned on me like the rest of the town."

He smiles, his hand slightly shaking as he lifts the cup to his mouth. It always does when he lifts something heavier than air.

"I know you didn't kill Marco," his gentle voice replies.

Relieved by his words, I go back to happily drinking my tea feeling it warm me from the inside. A few moments later, I straighten up in my seat.

"Wait, how are you so sure?"

"Because I've known you since you were a girl. The rest of the town only knows what you show them."

I raise my nose up in the air, faking snootiness. "A baker with a short-temper?"

"A woman who tries too hard."

His response instantly humbles me. I slump in my chair. To cheer me up, he leans forward to whisper conspiringly.

"And because I have an inside source at the precinct."

"Really?" I perk up, "Who?"

"Sadie Williams."

"The sunny detective?"

He grins at the nickname. "She is my granddaughter."

The kind detective is Mr. Williams's granddaughter. I wonder how and why I didn't put it together earlier. As I'm thinking of putting it together, an idea strikes me with the force of a steam engine.

"Mr. Williams, I have a huge favor to ask of you."

Chapter 4

Chapter 4

I'm leaving the room when my gaze falls on the mirror. A cream silk shirt tucked into a maroon pleated skirt over sheer tights and ankle boots. That's my outfit for today. My hair is in a bun, bangs loose on my forehead. It's more or less how I usually dress. Like they say; dress classy and be sassy.

A woman who tries too hard.

Walking back into my closet, I change my outfit and come back out.

The lavender cardigan (one of my favorites), jeans, and sneakers are a far cry from my previous outfit. I release my hair from the bun and leave it open in natural waves down my back.

"Not trying too hard now, am I?"

Loki slowly blinks at me from his position on the bed. I take that as a nod of approval from him and make my way to the kitchen.

Within thirty minutes, I'm at Mr. Williams's house. I never knew he lived so close to my parents' house. He has a porch full of colorful bird houses. Bathed in the cool sunlight, they look gorgeously vibrant. The door opens before I can knock.

"Hello there," Mr. Williams greets me warmly like he didn't just see me yesterday.

"You have a beautiful home," I compliment him after we're seated in the living room.

"My Edna would've been over the moon to hear that."

"She was a sweet woman."

"You remember her?"

I am surprised by his incredulity.

"Of course. She used to suggest good books to me over the summer break. And this one time I found a kitten in the street and we took him to the vet together. She told me about a hundred facts about cats. I think that's the afternoon I really realized that I love them."

His round nose is a light shade of red as he dabs at his eyes.

"Oh Lily," he sniffs. "It means so much to me that she is a part of your good memories."

I lean forward and squeeze his hand. "So are you."

He adorably huffs and sniffles into his handkerchief.

"You're very kind, child, kinder than this town deserves."

His words prompt me to ask the question that has been on my mind since yesterday.

"Mr. Williams, why are you helping me?"

He nods like he expected me to ask.

"Hillgrove is a lovely place. I have seldom felt the need to leave it. However, the only times I have, it has been because of people who think that they can impose their opinions on other people just because they are part of the same community. Edna and I were both seventeen when she got pregnant. You can imagine better than most how people must have talked. We were slandered worse than a corrupt politician. We lost our baby because of the stress and anxiety it caused her. It took some time to collect ourselves, but we got married soon after. We had our first daughter the year after. Our son, Sadie's father, two years after that. Only now, the town proclaimed us the picture-perfect happy couple. It made us so mad and we promised ourselves that we wouldn't let them get the best of us again and would live our life according to our own terms. And we did."

I have no words to put my feelings into. I had no idea about any of this.

"The reason why I agreed is because for some bizarre reason, you want the townspeople to actually like you."

He shakes his head in disbelief when I smile. It's the only thing I can do, knowing he wouldn't understand the bizarre reason.

The bell rings. He stands and excuses himself, telling me to remain seated. But when he opens the door and I hear Sadie's, Detective Williams's, voice I shoot to my feet.

"Hey Gramps," she hugs him.

"How are you, kiddo?"

I try to stay out of sight as long as I can, to give Mr. Williams time to explain my presence to her. However, being a detective, she spots me the minute she steps into his house.

"Miss Grayson," her eyes widen in surprise but she keeps herself calm and collected.

I need to learn how to do that. Her hair is in a ponytail and she looks a lot younger in her casual attire than she does in her work clothes.

"Call me Lily, please."

She looks at her grandfather, questioning him silently. He smiles innocently.

"Come in, come in," he ushers her into the living room. "We'll sit and have tea with the delicious cookies Lily brought."

"Yes, tea," she nods, then gestures to Mr. Williams towards the kitchen, "why don't we both go and prepare it?"

He shakes his head. "I can ring Donald—"

"No, no, we can do it," she links her arm with his and takes him to the kitchen.

She whispers to him as soon as they're out of my line of sight. Though I can hear them clear enough through the thin walls.

"Grampa, do you have no regard for your safety? She could be a murderer!"

"How do you know?"

I smile at the old man taking a stand for me.

"Do I really have to remind you? She's a suspect in the murder of Marco Sanchez."

"So am I."

"Gramps."

"Sadie, just hear her out. She's a good kid. You both have more in common than you know."

The silence that stretches tells me that Mr. Williams has succeeded in convincing Sadie even before she speaks.

"One wrong move and she's out."

"Go sit, I'll bring tea. She made almond and raisin cookies."

"You're evil."

I pretend to look outside the window when she returns.

"See anything interesting?"

I turn to her slowly. "Just the rumors about and around me."

Her eyebrow raises in surprise. She clearly wasn't expecting me to jump straight into it.

"Miss Grayson, I don't—"

"I only respond to Lily."

Narrowing her eyes, she continues, "*Lily,* I don't know what my grandfather said to you or why you're here, but whatever it is, my answer is no."

"He didn't promise me anything. I asked him to help me meet you outside the precinct. That is all."

"Why?"

I look at her crossed arms and take a deep breath.

"Because I want to help with the investigation."

A beat of silence passes. She bursts out laughing. I blink at her. Another beat passes. She stops laughing.

"Oh, you're serious."

"As a heart attack."

Her forehead knits together, "I don't understand."

I scoot forward in my seat, understanding that I have to sell it to her. Luckily, I'm good at that.

"My reputation is on the line here. I didn't kill Marco. So, anyone who is actively investigating me, is wasting their time." She opens her mouth to protest but I keep speaking, "I know my word amounts to absolutely nothing, but you can hook me to one of those lie detector machines and you'll know I'm telling the truth."

She holds up a hand, "There are multiple ways to outsmart those machines. I wouldn't lead an investigation with that."

"But that's just the thing, you're not leading an investigation, are you?"

I hold my breath and watch the color rise to her cheeks. *Got her.* She's smart, but she's also inexperienced. I have my flaws too. I just have learned to hide them well.

"This is the second time you have insulted me in the past minute," she speaks through gritted teeth.

"I know how hard it is to survive a male-dominated line of work," I push forward when she relaxes a little. "It doesn't take a genius to see that this is a test that they might want you to fail. *I* don't. I want *you* to be the one who arrests the murderer, not Detective Roberts or whatever his name is."

"He's actually the only one who treats me like an equal. So, I don't really see how you can help me better than him."

"I can be your eyes and ears on the ground. No offense, but people don't really like talking to the police. I don't know if you've noticed, but I don't."

She snickers, "Trust me, I have."

I huff and playfully roll my eyes. "It's not my fault you guys have such a daunting environment."

"Try going there for work every day," she mutters.

"I'll stick to my bakery. Thank you very much."

Our conversation sparks something. I realize I could be friends with her. Coming from me, that's a big realization. What's more is that she's looking at me with the same look on her face.

"I—"

"Do—"

We both start at the same time and share a laugh.

"I'm sorry. You go first," I say.

She waves her hand noncommittally, "I have heard a lot about you over the years from Gramps. I know you're a good person. But sometimes good people do bad things."

"Bad things, yes. Murders, no."

Her mouth tips up in a smile that she tries to smother. Just then, Mr. Williams returns with the tea. He winks at me when she isn't looking, his way of telling me that he purposefully took so long to give us more time to talk. I mouth a 'thank you'. Remembering the box of almond and raisin cookies I baked at his behest, I open it and place it on the table next to the tea.

"Here you go, Mr. Williams. I'm so sorry I had to remove them from the product list at the bakery. But no one bought it except you. I assume they're your favorite?"

The two share a look, with Detective Williams mainly glaring at her grandfather.

"For me," she speaks up, "he used to buy them for me."

Mr. Williams is far too pleased with himself when he announces, "They're *her* favorite, you see."

He bribed his own granddaughter for me. I fold my lips inside to hold in the laugh. What is it about old people that is so endearing?

"I hope you enjoy the cookies Detective Williams," I stand up, looking at the time.

"You're not staying for tea?"

I smile at the dear old man, "I have tea with you every other day, Mr. Williams. Thank you for today. I'll see you at the bookstore."

"Alright honey. Take care now,"

"You too. Goodbye, Detective."

I wave at them. Mr. Williams waves back while the detective sits with a cookie in hand, deep in thought. I walk out. It's a lovely day. I look around as I amble slowly down the street, counting my steps. *Come on, girl...* Four houses down, right as I am about to turn the corner, I hear a door open and slam shut.

"Lily, wait!"

Yes! I turn around, not having to act surprised because honestly it was touch-and-go for a moment. She runs up to me and I meet her in the middle.

"Is everything okay, Detective Williams?"

She smirks, "I only respond to Sadie."

And just like that, it's the start of a potential friendship for me.

Chapter 5

Chapter 5

I wake up with only one thing on my mind. Sadie had said that we need something solid, and I am more than determined to find it. If there is one person who I know is capable of physically hurting someone, it's Cora. So, that's exactly where I'm going to start.

Deciding to forgo my morning run for today, I take a while to myself. After a long bath, I spend an hour styling my wet hair. I usually wash it in the evenings so I don't have to rush. It brushes my lower back and is a pain to manage, but I love my hair. When I'm done with the blowout and straightening my bangs, I put on a black turtleneck sweater and black satin skirt. One glance at the mirror shows me that it is the perfect outfit for laying low.

In any place except Hillgrove.

I sigh and change my clothes again. I come back wearing a forest green cable knit sweater with jeans. I leave it untucked like all the other women in town. A groan escapes me at the sight. My clothes are wearing me instead of the other way around. The only saving grace is my hair.

"Loki, I look like a potato sack, don't I?"

He raises his head from where he's lying in his bed at the sound of his name. Seeing that there's no treats in my hands, he goes right back to sleep.

"Good talk, buddy."

Eyeing the containers of all the batters I prepared last night, a longing for my car hits me. I sold it three months ago to pay Marco a sum enough for him to hold the other shop for me. The jeep wasn't much but it was the first car I ever bought with my own savings. Knowing the containers wouldn't fit on the bicycle, I walk out and make my way next door. Polly will surely lend me her car for the day. She is always happy to help because she rarely ever needs her Mini.

I don't need to check my watch to know that she is done with watering her plants. Her garden is buzzing with life. She waters the flowers every morning and the vegetables every evening. The sound of the doorbell echoes outside as I press the round button.

"Coming!" she yells from somewhere inside the house.

I lean down to take a whiff of the jasmines planted close to her door. The cool, refreshing scent fills my lungs and puts a smile on my face. It stays there until the door opens just enough for Polly to jut her head out.

I awkwardly wave my hand in the air, "Uhh, hi."

With her lips pressed thin, she just nods.

"Are you okay?" I ask, slightly alarmed by her distressed look.

She eases up just a bit but still doesn't open the door. "Fine, fine. What's up?"

My brows furrow at her weird demeanour.

"May I borrow your car for the morning? I need to drop some stuff off at the bakery."

She loses the color in her face.

"Actually," she begins after a moment of silence, catching speed with every word, "I have somewhere to be in a few minutes. So if you don't mind."

I stare at her for a second, wondering why she is being like this. She still hasn't even opened her door. And now she's lying. *Why?*

"Sure. Thanks anyway."

I am walking down the pebble stone pathway through the garden when she calls out. I turn to face her. She is now standing outside her door, wringing her hands.

"Yes?"

"Did you—"

"Polly?" I prompt after she shakes her head.

"Did you really do it?"

I frown, trying to think about what she could be asking, but come up with nothing.

"I'm sorry. Do what?"

"Kill Marco," she blurts out.

I almost stagger back in shock. *That's* what all this was about? Is that what she thinks of me? Two years I've been her neighbour. We've had countless dinners together. I'd say she's almost my friend. Well, I would have, before now.

Squaring my shoulders, I relax my tight jaw enough to speak.

"I don't know. Did I?"

Leaving her shocked, I stride to my door and slam it behind me. Taking all my containers, I shove them, *carefully*, inside a travel bag. Then pick up my backpack and leave for the day.

The ride to the bakery is treacherous but I make it without the travel bag tipping over the bicycle or me with it. I stop in front of the back door and put the bag on the ground while I unlock the door.

I have barely seen Max in the last two days. He texted once, apologizing for his behaviour the other day. When I replied with different timings for us both, he didn't reach out again. So many years of our friendship, and he still doesn't know that I didn't actually want space, I just wanted him to try harder. Whenever I hurt someone, I have trouble sleeping until I make it right. He just never cares.

Switching on the lights, I make haste to take out mold trays and pour the batter in them. If I hurry, I can save an hour of prep before opening time and use it for investigation instead. Once the trays are in the oven and the second batch is ready on the shelf, I take off. There is a stillness to the area this early in the morning. People have yet to sidle out of their houses for the day.

I cross the street and skip an alley before turning into the next one. The protective netting overlooks Cora's nursery. I look for a way around it. If I can get into the nursery, I can surely get into her shop. Any sort of clue could push me in the right direction.

I notice a hole in the fence close to the ground. Made maybe by a cat or dog, most probably a dog judging by the size. Hands on hips, I suck in a breath as I look sideways. All clear. *It's now or never, Lils.* I lean down and start to plank my way through the space, careful not to get my jeans dirty and have to explain it later on. The jagged wire snags onto my sweater.

"Crap," I mutter as I back out of the hole.

There's a tear in my sweater. I groan and take it off. I wore this to lay low, not to gain attention with gaping holes. Tying it around my waist, I try again. This time the fence scratches at my arms, but I persevere and get to the other side.

I am immediately hit by the smell of greenery; musty and sweet. My vision is blessed with flowers of different colours, blooms of different sizes, hanging vines creeping from wall to wall. It is an enchanting place. Far better and more advanced than Polly's little garden. One I would've undeniably loved to spend lots of time in if it didn't belong to my only nemesis.

Clumsy in the heat of the moment, I knock over a pot. I bend down and put it back in the right place. The door to the shop is on the other side of the nursery. I'm surprised to notice that she even has the space to have a greenhouse right beside the nursery. She certainly pays more rent than I do. And as far as I know, the Reynolds aren't as loaded as they exhibit themselves to be. I stick to the cemented part of the ground, careful not to leave any behind footprints in the soil, and move towards the door.

Sending a quick prayer to the lord of justice, I twist the doorknob. A squeal of delight almost slips my mouth when it rotates all the way around. I step inside her shop for the first time ever. Not paying attention to the shelves and everything on display, I rush to behind the counter. The computer is powered off, the drawers locked.

"Dammit!"

Goosebumps erupt on my skin as the adrenaline wears off, leaving me cold. I walk to the coffee table, sifting through the books to see if there's maybe a paper she left behind in them. But they're all unused. Except one. I pick up the only book with a damaged spine.

'Death in the Garden: Poisonous Plants and Their Use Throughout History'

I put it back in its place, and take out my phone to take a picture of the incriminating book. When my screen doesn't light up, I hold the power button, only for it to die again. I curse at myself, remembering I didn't charge it last night.

All of a sudden, I hear the voice I absolutely do not want to hear right now, or ever. Instinctively, I crouch low, before turning around and peeking out of the blinds. Cora is right outside the door, talking on the phone. I stay there, trying to make out her words.

"Nope, been there done that. The bitch is still a thorn in my side."

I frown, *who is she talking about?* I quickly realize I don't have the time to stick around to find out, when I hear the keys jingling. Stealthily, I leap towards the other door and barely make it out as she enters the shop. Before I can run away, her words stop me in my tracks.

"Charlie you don't understand! I messed up with Marco. I never—" she sighs loudly and dumps her stuff on the counter.

With my heart thumping violently against my ribs and my hands covering my mouth, I struggle to get any air in. She killed Marco. *Oh my god*. She really killed Marco.

"I know. I'll be careful this time."

Knowing I have no means to record her, my trembling hands turn my sweater around to the front of my legs to camouflage behind the shrubs. The best thing I can do right now is escape. *Alive*. Wiping the tears from my eyes, I slither against the wall towards the fence. I'm almost there when she walks out too.

My arms ache from numbness as I stand there trying to decide whether to gun it or wait her out, while watching her from behind the plants. If I can see her, then at any given moment, she could see me too.

Decision made, I nod to myself.

Taking a deep breath, I do indeed gun it. Much to my horror, I bump into the damned pot again. Ignoring her shriek of surprise, I dive through the hole in the fence and run away as fast as I can. My sweater comes loose. I catch it before it lands on the ground. When I look back up, my eyes land on an old woman staring at me from across the street. I realize I must look like a madwoman to her. I slow down to a quick jog, controlling my flailing limbs, and put my sweater back over my tank top. Fully clothed, I try to get a handle on my breathing, still power jogging back to my safe haven.

The second I turn the corner, I run into someone and stagger to a halt. As their hands reflexively grip my upper arms, I hiss in pain.

"Miss Grayson, are you okay?"

I look up at Detective Roberts, and realize I'm way too close to his face. I quickly move out of his grasp, taking a deep breath through the burning pain in my arm. It must be a cut from the fence.

"Yes," It comes out as a gasp. I clear my throat and run a hand through my hair, praying that it looks tame enough.

He nods, but his scrutinising eyes remain on my hand, that I've now realized is trembling. I cross my arms over my chest. It occurs to me that this is the first time I've seen him standing. He is even more commanding now than he is in an interrogation room. His head tilts to the side, his eyes on my clothes for a split second before he looks back at my face. I glance down to see if anything is out of place, but don't notice anything.

"What can I do for you, detective?"

"I need to have a look inside your bakery," with his hands in his pockets, he tilts towards my shop. "If you would be kind enough."

Like I have a choice. I take the lead without answering him. If he wants to waste time looking around my shop while the real killer is right next door, he can be my guest. I'm going right to Sadie after he leaves.

Unlocking the door to the front, I enter the shop first and switch on the lights. Max did a good job of cleaning up after closing. The shop smells nice. I turn around to face the detective. He looks out at the street through the window, before turning to me.

"Don't you prepare fresh batches before opening time?"

"I do."

He quirks an annoying eyebrow in my direction. "Where were you just now?"

"Running an errand."

"Care to share?"

I don't break eye contact with him as I come up with an excuse.

"I forgot my phone charger at home."

"Your bicycle was here."

"I ran."

He says nothing, just looks down at my heeled boots. When his intense eyes come back to mine, I just offer him the iciest smile I can manage, hoping he has a brain freeze. He just smiles and points behind the counter.

"The back, through here?"

"Yes."

I move to the side to let him pass. He walks ahead into the office first. I don't know why I notice he has a very peculiar gait. It's hardly noticeable. I'm looking at his legs when he turns back around.

"The kitchen?"

Heat floods my cheeks. I turn around to open the kitchen's door. My oven is off; the thirty-minute timer is completed. I look at the clock, shocked to see the time. Detective Roberts inspects the kitchen and opens the back door to the alley.

"If you don't mind Detective, I have to open soon and I'm running a bit late."

"Sure," he closes the door and walks to the other one.

I don't bother following him out. Taking out the trays from inside the oven, I open the refrigerator to get the frosting for the cupcakes.

"Miss Grayson?"

I look up to see him still standing in the doorway, his black hair appearing blue under the lights.

"Yes?"

"You need security."

I nearly drop the tray in my hand. "What?"

"Cameras, out in the alley for the back door and one at the front. Inside the shop too, I'd recommend. And keep your window in the office locked."

"But— I've been here for two years. There's never been a single break-in."

He shrugs his broad shoulders, "Things change, Miss Grayson. Have a good day."

Chapter 6

Chapter 6

I pace the floor of Mr. Williams's living room, ferociously rubbing my forehead, unable to get Cora's words out of my head.

"You heard her correctly? Are you sure that's what she said verbatim?"

I halt in my tracks to look at Sadie. "I wouldn't blame her without cause."

"I'm just making sure," she shrugs, but her eyes stay focused on me. "I heard about an altercation between you two on the street."

"You'll hear about plenty," I say truthfully, "There's no love lost between us. But I never thought she'd really be capable of something so malicious."

Her ponytail swishes at her back as she shakes her head. "Let's not jump to any conclusions so quickly. Her words weren't a confession. She didn't clearly say that she killed Marco. So there's a million things she could've meant."

I pinch the bridge of my nose. I really thought that she would be with me on this.

I turn to her, arms akimbo. "Do you have any better ideas? I'm sure you guys have your own share of suspects. So, let's hear them."

She scratches at her ear, eyes flitting to the side. "Well, we're currently looking at Frank, Cora, and... you."

"*Me?*" I ask, surprised that they're still on my back.

"Yeah. That is why I need you to stay away from sleuthing around while you're under observation."

"Is that why Detective Roberts was sniffing around my shop today?"

Her brows knit together. "He was? By himself?"

I'm surprised by her confusion. I thought they ran everything by each other.

"Yeah, he was alone. But—" I stop as I remember what he said.

"What?"

"He told me I need cameras. A security system."

We're both frowning for different reasons when it strikes me.

"Did he say that so you guys could have a record of my whereabouts? Is that what this is about?"

She stands up from the couch, picking up her jacket from the back.

"Do you mind if I excuse myself for the day? You can stay here if you want."

With Mr. Williams at the bookstore, I didn't want to intrude.

"I should get going too."

She nods and I pick up my sweater.

"Remember what I said Lily. The police are on your tail. Just stick to your normal routine for now."

"What about Cora?"

"I'll look into her personally. Don't worry about it."

"Thanks Sadie. And for this as well." I lift my injured upper arm that she cleaned and bandaged while I told her what happened.

She smiles and leaves. I put on my sweater, mindful of the bandage.

"Miss Lily?"

I turn around. Donald, Mr. Williams's housekeeper, stands at the end of the corridor with his head bowed sheepishly.

"Yes?"

"I— It might not make a difference, but I know for sure that you didn't have anything to do with it. With Marco's death. And I'll tell anyone who says otherwise."

Warmth overloads my heart. I step up to him and wrap my arms around the small, chubby man.

"Thank you, Donald. It makes all the difference to me."

He sighs and pats my back before I release him and step out. The sun is setting. I sigh at the loss that was today. Tomorrow will be better I hope.

***

I wake up to Loki's loud meows in between '*zoomies*'. Remembering what Sadie said about sticking to my usual schedule, I decide to take him with me on my morning run. I pick up his retractable leash and put on my shoes. When he's finally strapped in after a game of hide and seek around the house, I step out with him.

Only to stop for a second. *What is Max's car doing here?*

I walk down my driveway and glance inside. He is snoring in the backseat, his legs over the console. I knock on the window. He doesn't even budge. A chuckle escapes me. He does sleep like the dead. I decide to let him sleep some more and turn to find Loki rubbing himself on the grass. I bend down to pet him but he takes off. So do I.

I have to sprint harder to keep up with him, but I like the challenge. When we reach the stream, Loki slows down to a crawl and ultimately just sits down to observe everything, his pupils blown wide. I settle down beside him to catch my breath.

An eerie feeling creeps up my neck. I look around to find the cause. It feels like someone is watching me but I don't see anyone. Uneasy to stay any longer, I stand up and scoop Loki into my arms. With measured steps, I walk out of the forest and back to my house.

Max is sitting on my porch step, rubbing his eyes, a makeshift tiny bouquet in his hand. He stands up straight when he sees me, all sleepiness gone. My heart softens. I was planning on playing a little tough. But to hell with that. I missed my friend.

I place Loki on the ground. Max extends the flowers to me.

"Do you think your neighbor will mind?"

"She thinks I killed Marco." I click my tongue, trying to mask my pain with a smile, and take the flowers from his hand.

"Damn, should've taken more," he smiles, then sighs exasperatedly. "I'm sorry, okay? About *how* I said what I said. I just want you to stay out of trouble. Is that really bad?"

Seeing Loki scratching on the mat outside the front door, I move past Max to open it. I do my best to not be disappointed by his apology. It's not like this is the first time.

Once Loki's in, I turn to Max, to find him still standing on the step.

"Aren't you coming in?"

He smiles and follows. I make us breakfast, his favorite bacon and eggs, while he watches from the bar stool. Keeping an eye on the time, I work at top speed.

"Lilly, slow down. Listen to me."

I sigh, "I'm not mad at you anymore, Max."

"I know," he shrugs like it's obvious. "That's not why I'm asking. I have something to tell you."

His somber tone pauses my movements.

"What is it?"

He sighs, "I was holding off telling you for as long as I could, but I know you'll check the records tomorrow."

"Max."

"No one is buying our bread," he admits. "I made the usual batches the first day and by closing time, I sold only three small breads. The next day I baked half the usual number and didn't sell any. And last night there wasn't a single customer!"

I grab his arm. "What did you do with the leftovers?"

His lips purse as he gives me a look, "I gave them at the shelter. *Duh.*"

I sigh in relief and stand up. "We'll figure something out, Max. I'm not going to shut down my shop just because we're facing a few problems."

"It's not just 'a few problems' though," he curls his fingers in the air. "We'll be bankrupt in no days."

"I'll make sure that we're not. Trust me," I offer him a reassuring smile and try to internalize it to myself as well, knowing full well that I am two blows away from having a mental breakdown.

***

Turns out, I should've searched for a therapist the day Max broke the news to me.

It has been three days since then and we haven't had any customers. We've stopped baking and are saving our ingredients but we still haven't gained back the losses incurred since Marco's death.

Here I was thinking of extending my business.

Max drums his fingers on the table. I flick another page of my book without reading a single word, my mind a thousand miles away from here.

"How long do you think we should wait before closing shop today?"

I glance at the clock, before answering him.

"It's only three p.m."

"We've been here since nine."

I raise an eyebrow at him.

"Well, *I've* been here since nine," he quickly corrects.

"It makes no difference Max. Even if no one comes, I'll keep the shop open for the usual timings."

When he doesn't argue, I look up from my book. He is focused on something outside the window. I turn around in my seat to look outside as well. A group of people are bustling across the street; taping and distributing flyers in the street.

We both walk out together. I watch as each shop in the street is visited by an individual handing out flyers, each shop except ours.

"Is it just me or are they avoiding us?"

"They're definitely avoiding us," I reply

To my surprise, Rhea is among the group. She turns away as soon as we make eye contact.

"I can't believe this." I shake my head in disbelief. "Mr. Williams was right about the people of Hillgrove."

Max elbows me, trying to lift my spirits. "We can always move back to Paris."

"Not a chance," I shake my head. "I'm going to set things right, no matter what it takes."

Chapter 7

Chapter 7

It is heartwarming to see how the town has really showed up for Marco. Even though no one personally handed me a flyer for his memorial, I found enough of them stapled around town. Fidgeting with the box in my hand, I search for the serving table among the throngs of people who are yet to be seated.

Startled when someone touches my arm, I look up, surprised to see Marco's wife in front of me out of all people.

"Here," she gestures somewhere behind her, "I'll put it with the rest."

"It's carrot cake," I say as I hand it to her.

She stops in her tracks, staring at the box with her head lowered. I don't have to tell her the reason behind it.

"Marco's favorite," she mutters.

I have a hundred questions I want to ask her. But I regress, as this is neither the place nor the time.

"I'm sorry for your loss, Hannah."

She glances at me, blinking back tears. "Thank you, Lily. I know he gave you a hard time but I hope you that know he cared about you."

I duck my head as my own eyes water. This damned town hadn't even given me the time to grieve him properly. She pats my shoulder and leaves me to my own devices. I wipe the unshed tears and turn my brave face on. Sure enough, there are countless people staring at me. I tug my long, black coat tighter around me and walk forward.

The wall is strewn with pictures of Marco and his family. I smile as I see a picture of him in his office, a scowl on his face as he looks straight at the camera. I can almost hear his voice in my head, demanding me to make more money.

I take out my phone and my thumb traces a path it knows too well by now. The picture of Marco and me in front of the bakery lights up my screen. It was the day of our agreement. We're both grinning, like we had a shared secret that no one knew about. And we did.

My eyes bug out of my head as I read the amount mentioned on the small piece of paper.

"Mr. Sanchez, I hope you don't mind, but I asked around to get an idea of the rent of this area. This isn't even half of what I was told."

He takes the paper from my hand and puts it back in his pocket, sliding the agreement towards me which mentioned the sensible amount that I had been informed about.

"It is what you will pay me for the first three months. Deal or no deal?"

Stupefied to my core, I gawk at him. "But... why?"

"When I was young, an Italian man trying to make his place on American soil, all I had wanted was for someone to give me a chance to prove myself. Sadly, no one did. Today I am giving you a chance. Because I feel that you are different, and tomorrow, you'll do your best to pay it forward."

Jutting my chin up to mask my trembling mouth, I extend my hand to him.

"Deal."

He smiles as he gives my hand a firm shake.

"All the best to you, Lily."

I squeeze his hand, "Thank you. For everything."

Feeling the wetness, I swipe at my face to wipe the tears trickling down. I put my phone back inside my pocket.

"Putting on a show for the people? Let me just tell you that no one is interested in watching you."

I take a deep breath before facing the council member with a smile. Of course. It's Tom's aunt.

Behind her, giving the perfect image of lap dogs, Tom and Rhea stand with their heads lowered. I haven't really interacted with Tom that much, but for Rhea to side with them is devastating.

"Cat got your tongue?"

My eyes return to the smirk on her face. She looks too smug after insulting me. I don't want to create a scene but I also can't let her get away with it.

"I'm here for Marco, not to address baseless and unwarranted opinions about me. Have a memorable day."

In the worst way, I angrily add in my head, as I march away from them. I shake my head. *I can't believe Rhea.* If a person who used to see me first thing every morning doesn't trust me, I don't expect other people to. But a little decency wouldn't hurt.

I spot an empty seat at the edge and hurry towards it. As soon as I sit, the man in the seat next to me stands up and leaves. I fist my hands in my pockets, wanting to clobber someone, or myself if it gets the edge off.

Hannah rises onto the stage, giving my anger a pause to simmer. While she speaks, my eyes scan the crowd. Max is sitting a few rows up with one of his gym fellows. The police are here too, positioned at the entrances and among the crowd. Though I can't see Sadie or Detective Roberts. My eyes stop at Polly, who is already looking at me with pitying eyes. *I guess I will find out the reason in the next second.*

My lungs burn with the need to scream when Cora steps onto the stage. She is the perfect image of misery, with hunched shoulders and red face. Wiping her nose with a tissue, she timidly approaches the mic, a paper in hand.

"Marco was a dear friend of mine." *A friend you might have killed.*

"I am honoured to have known him. He seemed fearsome but was always polite." *Polite, my ass.*

"I hope our capable detectives bring him closure by apprehending the killer soon. Just as well; diabetes is on the rise in our community." *Son of a—*

Unable to control myself, I shoot to my feet. Countless gazes swivel to me. Keeping her eyes on me, Cora folds her paper before ending her speech.

"I wish Marco peace wherever he is, and more strength to his family."

As she descends, people start murmuring to each other, pointing at me. With my nails digging into my palms, I stride to the front where she is.

This ends right here, right now.

Cora's face loses colour when she sees me approaching. I'm almost upon her when a hand grabs at my elbow. My dad's voice pulls me out of the red haze.

"Let it go, Lil."

I watch, heat pouring out of every pore, as she sinks back into her seat. With an arm around my shoulders, Dad turns me around and leads me away.

"Go back, Dad. I was just leaving."

He looks like he'll protest, so I step away from him.

"You sure, cupcake?"

I nod before leaving. Once I'm outside in the fresh air, I open my fist, the crescent shapes in my palm bleeding.

***

There's only one thing that would calm me down for sure. Since my bakery is closer, I go there to bake something to control my nerves. I park my bicycle and move to unlock the door, when I see it is already unlocked. That's strange. I pocket the keys and step forward, opening the door.

My heart stops the second I do. It plummets to the floor before coming right up to beat in my throat. My kitchen is in shambles. The place is completely turned upside down. Unable to tear my eyes away from the horror, I stay frozen in place until wetness on my cheeks breaks me out of the stupor.

I close the door. The bottom step looks like a good place to sit right now. I'm considering it when I'm called out.

"Miss Grayson."

I look up and see Detective Roberts walking into the alley. *I didn't call the police yet, right?* With his black hair and all black clothes, he looks more like an angel of death than a knight in shining armour.

"Good morning."

I nod, my throat still clogged with a huge lump.

"I'm sorry to drop in on you like this, so soon after the memorial. I went to the front but it was still closed."

He stares at me, waiting for me to say something. But my mind is numb, leaving my heart berserk. Who would do something like this? Did they trash the front too?

His gaze pins me in place as his brows furrow, "Are you okay?"

"The front is locked?"

He nods, "Yes."

"Did someone call you here?"

"No," his brows furrow, "Miss Grayson what is going on?"

"Then, I'm sorry, but why are you here?"

My eyes water again and I can hear the exasperation lacing my words. He must hear it too, because his keen eyes look around us, searching for anything to clue him in on what's going on.

"Detective Ro—"

"I came to give you this."

He takes out something shiny from his pocket and extends it to me. I look down. It's my bracelet. The one I dropped in the interrogation room. How did he find it after so many days?

"Thank you," I manage to whisper.

With tears swimming in my eyes, I attempt to close the clasp on my wrist three times before he steps forward, muttering a curse beneath his breath. Somehow, his bigger fingers nimbly manage the task in the first try without even touching my skin.

I try to breathe, but suddenly everything feels too heavy to handle.

Someone broke into my safe place and trashed it. I could've been inside.

I nearly keel over.

"Miss Grayson?"

"Someone broke in," I wheeze out.

He's immediately on guard. "Where?"

I turn around and open the back door. Within an instant, he steps around me and goes inside. I hear him talking on his walkie-talkie but it's all a blur. I lean against the wall next to the door and try to regulate my breathing. My mind wanders through every possibility. I even think of the expenses for the repairs. I open my eyes when I hear him step down in front of me.

"Did you have security cameras installed?" He asks, his voice urgent.

I shake my head. He tuts and rubs his forehead.

"Did you see someone when you came here? Or someone suspicious on the way here?"

I shake my head again.

"When did you arrive?"

"A couple of minutes before you."

"Did you touch anything inside the kitchen?"

"Just the handle."

"It's not broken," he states. "Someone used a key. Who else has a copy?"

"Max and umm... Marco."

"You *need* a security system," he emphasizes. "This is not safe, Miss Grayson. You could've been inside. Do you have someone to handle it for you?"

"I can do it myself."

He shakes his head, mumbling to himself and pulls out his phone, walking a few feet away.

"Lily!"

I turn at the sound of my name to see Max jogging towards me. He stops short a foot away, spotting the detective.

"What is *he* doing here?"

"Max—"

He cuts me off after glancing into the kitchen.

"What the hell?"

He steps inside to take a closer look.

"Don't touch anything," I warn him.

He comes out and holds me in a hug. I convince myself to take comfort in it.

"Please tell me you're not hurt." His words are muffled into my hair.

"I'm okay," I say and step back when I hear a throat clear.

Detective Roberts looks between the two of us. I glance back at Max, and am surprised by the hostility on his face.

"Hello Mr. Sloan. Do you mind answering some questions?"

Max squares his shoulders, "Not at all Detective."

They step away just as a cop car arrives at the mouth of the alley. I see Sadie get out with a couple of other officers. The ones with the bags go straight inside while Sadie stops next to me.

"You good?" She asks, her empathetic eyes much similar to Mr. Williams's.

I shrug, trying to curb the tears.

"Do you have any ideas about who it could've been?"

"I don't know. I don't even know why someone would do this."

"Could've been a rager, or just someone trying to get back at you for Marco."

A whine erupts low in my throat as tears escape my eyes, "But I didn't—"

"We know that," she whispers, "but the rest of the town doesn't. And now, after Cora's shout out, they're going to keep coming at you until they find someone else. You need to be prepared."

I shut my eyes and take a deep breath.

"Hey," she squeezes my shoulder, "you're fine. I know you're stronger than you look."

The two men return. I notice they're almost the same height, with Max being only a couple of inches taller. Sadie straightens up, barely acknowledging him.

"You should head home for the day," Detective Roberts addresses me. "We'll seal the place while we check for fingerprints and set up surveillance for the night."

"But I've never—"

"It's okay, Lily," Max gives me a reassuring smile. "It's for the best."

"Never what, Miss Grayson?" Detective Roberts urges me to finish my sentence.

"Closed my shop for a whole day in two years."

He glances at his partner. Sadie, miraculously understanding what he means, turns to me.

"If you feel up to it, you can come back later in the evening. But I don't think you'll be able to use the kitchen. So, if you want to sell something, you'll have to bake elsewhere."

I glance at Max. He knows there isn't any selling or baking to be done.

"You know what, I think I'll take the day off."

"Good call, Miss Grayson," she shoots me a reassuring smile.

The detectives leave me and Max alone. I grab my bicycle. Max stops me by a hand on the handle.

"Let's go have lunch."

"I might throw up." I say, still feeling sick to my stomach.

"Hot chocolate, it is then."

We walk to a nearby kiosk and grab hot chocolate before taking a seat on a bench.

"How are we going to pay for the repairs?"

I scrape off the sticker on the cup with my nail.

"I'll manage," I say after thinking it through.

"I can pay—"

"No." I refuse at once. We'd had this talk before. I didn't want any money from him. Or anyone, in fact. "Thanks, but I'll manage."

His head dips to the side as he looks at me. "You don't seem too affected by this."

My nails dig out of my injured palm as I flatten it against my knee. *Not too affected.* I cried thrice in the past thirty minutes, even though I'm not a crier, and he says I'm not too affected.

"You're right. I'm just pissed. I don't understand what I ever did to them to come at me like this."

"Maybe now they will back off," he shrugs.

"What do you mean?"

He puts aside his cup and turns to me. "Now the town will see you as a victim too, and they'll stop bullying you."

"Victim?" I gape at him. "Max, how can you think like that?"

"I'm not saying I'm glad for what happened, but it's not a loss either."

My lips pull down in a frown as I try to think of it his way. It feels like dirty politics.

I shake my head, "No Max, it is most definitely a loss. We weren't faring too well to begin with and now this added expense. It is a huge setback on my plans."

He sighs and puts an arm around my shoulders.

"It's okay, we'll go through it together, like we always do."

Chapter 8

Chapter 8

I am cleaning Loki's water fountain when the doorbell rings. The clock reads 6:50 a.m. I frown, thinking who it could be. Given how semi-social I usually am, and how notorious I am these days, no one comes to mind. Still, I put down the filter and tighten my robe as I have yet to get dressed after my shower.

Polly stands on my porch step with a vase in her hands. I cross my arms, not very happy to see her. She clears her throat, shifting on her feet.

"What do you want?"

She holds out the vase in her hand. Blue flowers peek out from the top.

"Blue hydrangeas," she offers me a small, sheepish smile. "They symbolize regret."

"Do they now?"

"I'm sorry, Lily." She sighs, scratching at her palm. "I shouldn't have doubted you. And I'm sorry for what happened at the memorial. Cora was way out of line."

"At least she's honest about her hatred for me. It doesn't disappoint me anymore."

Her face falls and I hate myself for hurting her. But I remind myself of how she hurt me and close the door on her face. Weeping silently, I go to my bedroom to get dressed. Loki finds me when I'm wiping my face and rubs himself against my legs, clearly sensing my distress.

"It's okay, Loki. I'm just finding out that people don't need reasons to blame someone, no matter how long they've known them."

He meows in response before jumping up to lie down at the foot of the bed. I put on my jeans and black turtleneck with black combat boots. The dark clothes match my mood at least.

When I reach my bakery, I find a huge man sitting on the stoop with a bag at his feet. He glances up and stands as soon as he sees me. I cautiously stop a few feet away as he does. He is really tall and built, his arms the size of my head that could easily squeeze the life out of me. With his afro cut closely to his head, and the sheer size of this man, I'm guessing he used to be a bodyguard.

"Miss Grayson?" His voice is deep and gravelly.

"Yes?"

"I'm here to set up your security system."

"Security system?" I repeat to confirm. "But I didn't call you."

"Roberts did," he picks up his bag. "If you don't mind—"

I instinctively step in as he advances towards the door to my bakery.

"Hold up. *Detective* Roberts?"

He glances down at my raised hands, then back at my face, making me conscious of how puffy it was because of all the crying.

"How many other Aiden Roberts do you know?"

Heat rises to my ears.

"Of course," I nod and unlock the front door.

He did say he'll arrange someone. But I didn't think he actually would. *How much do I have to pay this guy?*

"Where are you going to work right now?"

"Why do you ask?"

He deadpans, "To stay out of your way."

"Don't you have someone coming to help?"

"No."

We are at an impasse. If there was someone other than him, I would've busied myself with baking for them. Judging by his figure, I don't think he enjoys sweets. Still, I think it's best to ask.

"Would you like me to whip up something for you to eat?" His eyebrows raise in surprise at my question. "A croissant, muffin, cupcake, bis—"

"No," he stops me from listing more items. "Thank you."

"How do you like your coffee?" I ask.

"Black."

I nod to myself, having guessed his answer already.

"You can start anywhere you like."

I breathe in relief when he doesn't ask any questions and walks to the back. Busying myself behind the counter, I prepare our coffees. A drilling sound jars the walls.

Within no time, he is back out. He strides to the front door with a stepping stool in hand. After drilling, he steps down to pull a camera from his bag. Once he is done, he comes back inside.

I offer him his cup. He grunts and wordlessly goes to my office. *Wait.* My office? There's no need for a camera there. I follow him, about to call his name, when I realize I don't even know it.

"Hey, what's your name?"

He enters my office and powers up the age old computer that came with it.

"Do you use a laptop?"

"No, I had my friend update and install new software on this computer. It works just fine now."

He nods and starts typing away after the computer boots up. I wait for him to be done.

"Here you go."

I peek over at the screen. It shows surveillance from the two cameras.

"Personally," he points at the window. "I think you need one more outside this window and one over the counter overlooking the shop."

"Any other day, I would've told you that you're wrong. But after yesterday, I won't," I sigh. "You can do whatever you like. Just tell me how much I owe you."

He picks up his bag and walks outside, "Nothing. You don't owe me anything."

I frown. "What do you mean?"

He props up the stool behind the counter and starts drilling.

"I asked you something," I yell over the noise.

He puts the machine down and picks up a camera, screwing it in with another machine. Done with the task, he hops down. I step over at the only way behind the counter, blocking his path before he can grunt his way out again. He notices and sighs, putting his bag down and crossing his arms.

"Aiden is my friend. We have a tab. It's handled."

Aiden—*even his name is all strong and mysterious*. I shake my head and cross my arms too, though my arms are nowhere near the size of the man in front of me.

"Well, I'm not friends with either of you. I don't even know your name. So I'm not comfortable with not paying you."

He eyes the ceiling. "My name is Sam. I know you're Lily. I also know that Aiden will kill me if I take any money from you."

"It's not his call to make. I'll just keep asking until you tell me, Sam. How much do I owe you?"

His indifference melts into a smile, "You're really tenacious, aren't you?"

"So I've been told."

"Your oven's broken."

I falter as the realization hits me like a train. *Have I lost it?* I've been thinking of baking all morning. How did I forget that the kitchen was ruined yesterday? I rub my forehead, trying to gather my wits as the memory of my broken kitchen flashes in my mind.

"Forgetting details about a traumatic incident is normal," Sam reassures me. "I would've asked for banana bread as payment if your kitchen was in order."

"I make a mean banana bread," I admit dejectedly.

He smiles and picks up his bag again. "Tell you what, when your kitchen is up and working again, have Aiden bring it to me and we'll be even."

"You got it."

I get out of his way and he goes into the office again. Meanwhile, I make him a new to-go cup of coffee, and drink my own latte. I can't believe I forgot the state of my kitchen. The ovens were smashed in. They have to be repaired before I can use them again. I might need new ones. I sigh. The list of expenses just keeps growing.

He comes back a few minutes later.

"You're all set."

"Thank you, Sam. Would you like your coffee now?"

He grabs his cup from the counter and chugs half of it in one go. My jaw hangs open.

"Thanks for this," he raises the cup in the air, "needed it."

"Anytime," I mutter, still horrified by how he inhaled it.

"See you around," He gives me a two-fingered salute before walking out of the front door.

I'm still looking out, when a curvy blonde enters the shop, a thumb hooked over her shoulder.

"Who was that hunk?" Stella makes a show of fanning herself.

Delight takes my breath away and I gasp as I sprint to her. She giggles, wrapping her arms around me tightly.

"Damn bamboo, you miss me that much?"

My tear ducts decide to overflow at that very moment. When I choke on a sob, Stella grabs my shoulders to back me up.

"Are you crying?" Her face colours with shock and concern, "Why are you crying? What the hell happened?"

For once in weeks, I don't feel the need to hold back anything. I cover my face to muffle my cries, but still cry all my woes out in front of the one person I trust fully. She hugs me again and rubs my back, shushing me like she does while comforting Hazel, her one-year-old daughter.

"Come on, Lils," I come up for air as she drags us towards a nearby table.

She thankfully hands me a tissue before I wipe my tears and snot with my sleeve. Conjuring a water bottle out of her tiny bag, she hands it to me.

"Drink this, then start from the beginning."

***

I lean back in my chair, taking my first deep breath since I began speaking. Stella's face is red with anger, but she held it in while I was recapping everything since Marco's death.

"Do you wish to talk more?"

I shake my head. She nods, squaring her shoulders, getting ready to give me the full 'bff-analysis' as we like to call it.

"Okay, first of all, I'm sorry about Marco. I know how close you guys were, so if you ever need to talk, you know I'm always with you," she squeezes my hand on the table, before slapping it hard. "Second, you should've called me! I was in the Bahamas, not on the moon!"

"It was your first vacation since your honeymoon," I protest while rubbing my hand.

"Whatever! You still should've called."

"To have ruined your 'stress-free sunbathing while sipping on mojitos'?" I quote her. "No thank you. How was it by the way?"

Her eyes fall shut as she grins, "*The best.*"

"Yeah, I can tell by your glowing skin. Ryan to thank for that?" I tease her.

She blushes, "We're trying for another kid. I hope we have twins!"

I chuckle at her enthusiasm. She has wanted a huge family ever since I've known her, and I've known her since the fifth grade. Seeing how she is already an excellent mother, I can easily imagine her with more kids.

"You guys are great parents. I can't wait to be a godmother again."

She playfully rolls her eyes, "As if I would make you godmother again. You don't even call me when you're suffering."

Before I can speak, she raises three fingers.

"*Third*, when do I get to meet this Sadie? Fourth, you need to make things right with Polly."

My expression sours, and she raises her hands to placate me. "For multiple reasons. You would've known this, if you'd ever pay attention to my frequent tidbits of town gossip, that Polly was married to Frank, Marco's partner. They got divorced a few months back. People say that it was because Frank was cheating on her with Hannah, Marco's wife."

"Are you serious?" My eyes widen, "Hannah was devastated at the memorial. She couldn't have cheated on him."

"It could've been one way or the other. It's just hearsay," she shrugs.

I shake my head, "I can't believe the things people say in this town. Especially not after this whole ordeal. They've spread all kinds of rumours about me, Stel. According to them, *I* killed Marco. Even Polly said so!"

"Deny all you want, but the reason why you're so offended and hurt by her more than others, is because she *is* your friend. And what matters is that she apologized. So from the way I see it, it's your turn to make a move. Still, it's your call."

I cross my arms over my chest, "I'll go talk to her if I get the time."

She smiles, knowing I'll definitely talk to her, but doesn't call me out on it. Instead, she just leans on the table on her forearms, her smile turning salacious.

"And last but certainly not the least, you really should go thank Detective Roberts."

I scowl, "For what?"

Her smile drops and she drops her face into her palms. "Oh bamboo, you're clueless."

"About what?"

She raises her head, "The man held onto your freaking bracelet for days! He called his friend to install CCTV at your shop, which you have to show me of course, and he paid for it. Plus, he did all this *while* you're a suspect."

"Are you done?" I ask her calmly, causing her to huff. "It's nothing like what you're thinking. The reason why he was so adamant on the cameras is because it'll help them keep an eye on me, the *suspect*," I point at myself with my thumbs. I add, making a face, "Also, he is annoying and bossy."

"Have you looked in the mirror?" she deadpans.

I sigh, "I know I have been difficult to deal with since I moved back, but I really thought I'd *be somewhere* by now. Instead, I'm on the verge of being bankrupt with no source of income."

"You'll work it out, Lil," she keeps nudging my leg with her toe until I smile. "You always do. You just needed to let it all out. I'm sure you'll find things to be clearer now. Until then," she wiggles her eyebrows, "want to get back at Cora?"

"It's no use," I tut, "She'll find a way to spin it. She's got the whole town wrapped around her finger."

"Believe it or not, you have the benefit here. You spent a decade away from Hillgrove, half of which you were married to Cora's sorry twin. Charlie must have mentioned something that makes her tick. I know you don't like to think back on those years, but try to remember. Be innovative with the town as only you can, put it together with what annoys Cora, and voila!" she flourishes in the air.

I laugh at her antics. "I'll try my best."

"I know you'll do. You always do. Just try to have fun in the process, yeah?"

I know she's not just talking about getting back at Cora now.

"Stella—"

"Don't Stella me, Lily. When was the last time you went out? Had fun? Made friends? Went on a date? Do you even remember?"

I huff defensively, "I went out on New Year's."

"New Year's was four months ago."

I wince. *Walked right into that one.*

She deflates, her voice softening, "I'm just trying to make sure you don't die alone, bamboo."

"I won't, I'll have Loki."

"If he doesn't kill you first."

We both laugh. She's right. I do feel lighter. Things are mapping out in my mind. Warmth of hope blooms in my chest and I know I can help solve Marco's murder.

I know where to start again.

Chapter 9

Chapter 9

As I bake Polly's favourite red velvet cupcakes, I wonder why I didn't get around to baking sooner. I feel so much calmer now. Though, of course it is also linked with having talked to Stella. We both call each other our platonic soulmates. She is definitely my sister from another mother. I'm decorating the cupcakes when my phone rings.

Before I can even speak, Sadie launches into it.

"I just got your message. I'm looking into it. I'll let you know when I have something. Gotta go, bye."

I chuckle at the screen as she hangs up without listening to me at all. She sounded like she was in a rush, which given her line of work, I can understand. I put down my phone and get back to frosting the cupcakes.

Taking time off from the bakery is undoubtedly a good idea. I can bake at home whenever I want. I tell myself that with Loki keeping me company, this is more peaceful than baking at the bakery's kitchen. Once the plate of cupcakes is covered, I boop my little finger, the only clean one, on his nose.

"Thanks for watching today's episode of baking with Lily. Being the sole viewer, you get a special treat."

I open the packet of his biscuits. He sprints to me, nipping softly at my legs until I feed him. I pet his purring belly when he's done eating. After he struts away, I go get changed. Dressed for the day in my pleated brown skirt paired with a powder blue blouse, I put the next batter in the oven before leaving for Polly's.

She opens the door quickly, dressed in only a silk robe. She looks surprised to see me, looking behind me almost like she was expecting someone else.

"I hope I'm not intruding. These are for you," I offer her the plate. "Red velvet, your favorite."

"You didn't have to."

"I wanted to," I look at her, hoping she understands my intent. "I didn't feel too good about turning you away the other day."

"I would've done the same, maybe worse. Would you like to come in?"

"Sure."

She opens the door wider to let me in. The sweet scent of flowers floats in the air. I take a seat on the armchair by the window. It's where I usually sit when I come here because I can see her in the kitchen from here. It makes for easier conversation.

Which is how I see it when she loosens the knot on her robe and tugs it slightly down her shoulders before going to the fridge. I frown to myself. It isn't that hot today. I look down at my sleeveless blouse and knee-length skirt. Should I have worn something different for the day?

I am broken out of my musings when she returns and hands me a can of iced tea before sitting in the chair across from me with a cupcake in hand. She notices me smiling as she digs in.

Flushing, she swallows, "I would offer one to you but I know you don't like red velvet."

"You're right. Besides, these are only for you to enjoy."

"I'm glad you came, Lily," she sighs, leaning forward to squeeze my hand. I look away from her generous cleavage. "I know I was way out of line that day. But I heard rumours and was foolish enough to have considered them."

"You should have trusted me."

Knowing I wouldn't get a better opening than this, I proceed, with extra caution.

"You know, I've heard things about Hannah and Frank too, but I know better than to believe them."

Her attention suddenly locks on me. "What kinds of things?"

"I don't know if I should say," I shake my head.

"It's okay," she shrugs a shoulder. "Better from you than others."

I take a deep breath, hoping it doesn't hurt her. *I want to dig out the truth, but I also don't want to hurt her.*

"I heard that you and Frank got divorced because of cheating."

Her face pales and she stops breathing for a moment.

"Polly?"

She blinks repeatedly, lowering her gaze. "It's true."

Shock courses through me. I can't believe it. *Hannah was cheating on Marco?* My jaw tightens with anger on his behalf.

"Did Marco know?"

Her eyes whip to mine, a strange sharp look passing her features before mellowing. I wouldn't even have noticed if I wasn't looking closely.

"If he did, he didn't do anything about it."

"And you did?"

"I divorced my husband, didn't I?" She shrugs. "Haven't spoken to him since."

We sit in silence while my thoughts run wild. Although Stella had told me about this, I hadn't believed any of it. But for Polly to have confirmed it, I am shocked to know that it is indeed true.

"What are you thinking about?" she asks, putting her empty plate aside. She crosses her bare legs and turns to me fully. Her big, earnest eyes make me feel at ease. It is always easy to talk to her.

"I thought Marco and Frank were friends."

She scoffs, "My ex-husband is no one's friend. Be careful around him."

"Careful?" I lean towards her, "Polly, did he hurt you?"

She looks at me then, her eyes slowly roaming my face, before she gives me a sad smile.

"You too were married once, Lily. Did he hurt you?"

My heart stops in my chest. A grip on my throat tightens until I can't speak.

"Did he?" she probes at my wounds.

"More than anyone."

Appeased by my answer, she leans back in her chair. "I'm sorry."

I nod, "I'm sorry too."

***

During the ride to the precinct, I find myself taking empty streets so that no one sees me going there. The last thing I want right now is people starting rumours, especially not about this. I get off the bicycle and wipe my sweaty palms on a tissue, before straightening my skirt and taming down my bangs and ponytail. Deep breaths do little to calm my racing heart.

Why the hell am I so nervous? *He* is just a detective who thinks I killed someone. It's *totally* normal. I huff and pick up the bag from the basket. I don't care what he thinks about me. I'm only here to pay Sam back.

People start staring from their cubicles as soon as I walk in. I thought police officers are supposed to be discreet. I keep my head up as I walk to the receptionist.

"Hello. Can I see Detective Roberts please?"

I thank my lucky stars when the old woman gives me a pleasant smile and tells me where to go.

"Thank you, have a nice day."

She beams at me, "You too, honey."

Instantly feeling a million times lighter, I cross the hallway and turn right, like the lady told me to. I notice his office is right next to the chief's. Sadie's office isn't in the same corridor. I knock on his door. Hearing his muffled response, I open it and step inside. His table is brimming with files; some open, some closed. It is really dark in here during the daytime, only his table lamp lights up the space. His hair shines a dazzling chocolate shade under the golden light. I notice he is left-handed, as he scribbles something on a page.

"Hurry up," he says without looking up, still writing, "I don't have all day."

My mouth drops open. *Who does he think he is?* I step ahead and put down the bag right in his line of sight.

"I don't either."

His head swivels up, eyes widening when he sees me. With lightning speed, he shuts the file he was writing in, presses a button on his desk that turns on the lights in the office, and shoots to his feet, all at the same time. Nice to see I can surprise a smart man like him.

"Miss Grayson, what are you doing here? And what is this?" He waves his hand towards the bag.

"I didn't come here for an interrogation," I cross my arms. "You sent your friend to set up cameras."

A gleam pools his eyes as his head tilts to the side.

"Is there a question in there somewhere?"

Did he just— I try my best to curb my smile and narrow my eyes at him instead.

"You didn't have to make the payment. I am capable of handling my own finances."

He nods, "I don't doubt it."

I am surprised at his quick acquiescence. But before I can ask him what I have to pay, he jumps in.

"But I feel responsible for not ensuring you— I mean, your bakery, had enough security before somebody broke in. Think of this as penance for me."

"Do you expect a 'thank you' for it?" I frown at the strange man.

The corner of his mouth tips up, before he schools it. "Of course not. Now, may I know what this is?"

"It's for Sam. He told me he loves banana bread. So I baked it at home to return the favour. He said you'd take it to him."

This time, I can clearly see that he is failing at controlling a smile. "Awfully chatty, wasn't he?"

"He was perfectly fine." *Unlike you,* I add inside my head.

He finally grins. And I get why he doesn't go around flashing it to just everybody. It deserves to be a rare sight at a museum somewhere. Deep dimples peek out from beneath the light stubble on his cheeks, and his eyes crinkle adorably at the corners.

For the first time, it hits me how handsome he is.

"I'll personally take it to him, Miss Grayson, don't worry."

I open my mouth to thank him, but what comes out is, "You better."

Still smiling, he picks up the bag and sets it on the coffee table in the corner of his office. Come to think of it, that's the only empty surface in his whole office. I see no empty food containers. Where does he eat?

"Don't your eyes hurt?"

"What?"

Exactly— *what?* Why did I ask him that?

"Umm, you know," I struggle with my words, "because of how dark it was when you were reading."

"It helps me focus."

"Oh."

A whole wave of awkwardness wraps me up. More so, when I notice the smile on his face is gone and he is back to being the stoic detective. I shuffle on my feet while stepping back.

"I should get going. I'm sorry to have kept you from work."

"No worries," he nods.

I nod too. Then turn around to leave.

"Miss Grayson?"

I turn back rather quickly. "Yes?"

"Close the door on your way out."

Embarrassment flushes my blood with heat, but a twinge of anger replaces it within a second.

"Sure," I give him a saccharine smile. "Anything else?"

"No, thank you."

Still smiling, I open the door wide open, and leave it open behind me as I walk out into the hallway. The only con is that I can't see his face after. As I'm leaving the station, I bump into Sadie.

"Lily?" She steps back, surprised.

"Hi."

"What are you doing here? Is everything okay?"

"Yeah, everything's fine," I reassure her. "I'll tell you later."

She looks around at the prying eyes, then gestures for me to come with her. I follow her to her office. It is indeed not in the same corridor as the chief. She unlocks her door and switches the lights on. Her office is neat and meticulous, unlike the other one I was just in.

"Any lead on the break-in?"

She shakes her head, her eyes downcast. "I'm sorry Lily. The place was forensically swiped clean. Not one single print, not even yours. I don't think there *will* be a lead."

Even though my heart breaks that I will never know who trashed my kitchen, I put on a brave smile for her.

"Don't beat yourself up. Let's just focus on finding the killer."

She nods, but her guilt is evident.

"Did you do it?" I ask her about the text I sent her this morning to divert our minds.

I told her about Cora's probable financial problems, and how her family is deep in debts because of their father's gambling habit. She gestures for me to sit down. Once I am seated in front of her, she leans forward on her desk to whisper.

"She has a pretty solid alibi of that morning. I can't get into it without breaking a lot of laws, but please trust me on this. She found a way to make a lot of money and could do pretty well for herself if she didn't have to look after her father too."

I file away what she says to align everything about the Reynolds in my mind. It would be better if I could bring myself to not care.

"I talked to Polly today. She is Frank's ex-wife. They were married for about four years and got divorced because—"

"Hannah and Frank were secretly seeing each other?" She fills in, shaking her head. "I don't know why but I can't bring myself to believe it."

"I know right!" I lean in, glad that someone else feels the same as I do. "Something seems off about it. But Polly confirmed it today and I don't think there's a better source than her."

"I'll ask Aiden to look into this as well since he's the one working on Frank. Meanwhile, try your best to stay away from him because he's the prime suspect in my opinion."

Discomfort overcomes my senses. She's the second one to warn me against Frank today. I hope I don't have to see him any time soon.

Chapter 10

Chapter 10

ups & Cakes is officially closed until further notice.

I have newspapers taped from top to bottom of the windows so no one can peek inside. The secret project will take some time but I am confident that this is the best time to do it since we had no customers regardless. I told Max that I'm closing the shop temporarily but he can still drop in whenever he likes.

So now it's just me and a task that I should've completed ages ago. With all the doors locked and the surveillance up and working, I feel safe enough to work with my headphones popped in. I move to the beat as I dip the roller in fresh paint. My jumper is a mess by now but I don't care. Even if I had the money to hire professionals, I wouldn't have done it. Because this is something that I have wanted to do myself since I opened the bakery.

The second day, Stella joins me with her laptop to complete her work while I do the same.

"I feel high as a kite. I coded four apps in one hour." Stella proceeds to explain the coding to me and I've known her long enough to know that it is time to stop listening.

"I think it's the paint," I say, grinning at her, when she finally ends her rant. "I can't believe you're high on paint."

She yawns out her reply, tugging at the collar of her shirt. "And I can't believe you're remodelling the shop on your own."

"I'm not doing it on my own. Dad will be here later today to redo the ceiling. Once that's done, I'll hire someone to change the tiles. While they do the floor, I'll spray paint the furniture to match the theme."

"What about your kitchen?"

"I've sold a few things from home," I admit in a rush, hoping she doesn't berate me for it. "It's not like I have guests over often, I don't need so much furniture."

"Did you get a good deal?"

"Wait," I blink, "you're not going to school me about my 'pride' like everyone else?"

She rolls her eyes, "Unfortunately, I happen to know you. Also because I know *why* you are the way you are."

I stop painting and keep the roller down, before turning to her.

"Sadie told me that Cora still takes care of her deadbeat father."

Her brows pull down together and I wait for the penny to drop. She gasps when it finally does.

"What in the blazes did Charlie do with your money then?"

I shrug, "The last I heard, he was gallivanting with his third twenty-year-old girlfriend in Florida."

"Who does he think he is? Leo DiCaprio?"

Smiling at her reference, I pick up the brush again.

"Seriously, Lils, can I *please* just mess up his life just once? You know I can."

"Hacking your way into his measly life is way beneath your capabilities, Stel. I don't want you to do that."

The messy knot of blonde hair wobbles on top of her head as she furiously shakes her head.

"Lily, he stole your hard-earned money for years. The least I can do is put him on the no-fly list."

"According to the court, it wasn't stealing if it was from a joint account. They don't care that I thought I was helping him support his father. Besides, it was almost six years ago. I wouldn't even be thinking about it if I wasn't in such a pickle right now."

She sighs and turns her laptop towards me. The colourful screen draws me in and I go to take a closer look.

"It's for the bake sale. I figured if we want people to buy your products again, we need to show them what they're missing. So I made this brochure with all your best-selling desserts and I added the deals you sent me on the back."

I tap the key to turn the page to the back, where all the discount offers are mentioned in block letters. I only came up with the idea for a bake sale last night. Sure enough, the first person I called was Stella since she was the one who had ignited the thought process.

The bake sale—with all the proceeds going into the repair of the clock tower—is my way of taking the narrative back into my hands. Fingers crossed, I'll be able to engage the town in a good way. Plus, if it all goes as I expect it to, Cora will be pissed to not be the centre of attention.

To see my idea so attractively packed into a pamphlet encourages me more than I imagined it would. But at the same time, it scares me too. What if no one shows up? What then?

"Before either of us starts panicking, tell me the date I should write on this."

"Tomorrow?"

She stares at me, eyes wide and unblinking.

"What?"

"The day after is your birthday," she speaks slowly and clearly.

"So?"

"So heaven forbid tomorrow doesn't go well, you'd be setting yourself up for the worst birthday in the history of thirtieth birthdays."

I chuckle at her visible horror. "I'll be fine, Stella. It's just a bake sale."

The sudden sound of the lock being opened jolts us both. I hold up the paint roller in front of us as a weapon. The door opens and in walks Frank. Keeping in mind all the warnings I'd gotten against him, I don't lower the roller.

Frank smirks and lowers his sunglasses down the bridge of his nose, enough to peek over them.

"Preparing to send me wherever my friend is?"

I glare at him as I put down the roller and cross my arms.

"The shop was locked for a reason. You can't just use your key whenever you want."

He puts the said key in his pocket, and tugs at the lapels of his suit jacket. Stella powers off her laptop and stands up too. Though she doesn't look threatening at all in her polka-dotted shirt, he notices her backing me up and his neck tenses up.

"I only used my key because soon it will be the only one being used in this door. If you don't pay all the remaining rent within two weeks, that is."

I shake my head, "I had a deal with Marco—"

"That died when he did. Now, you have to deal with me. And I'm not Marco."

My gut tightens. He is right. He isn't Marco. He is far more cut-throat than Marco could ever be.

"I need some time."

"You've had enough time and coddling." He sneers at me, his moustache curling up. "I'm fresh out, so you ain't getting none from me. Clear this shit up and get to work. I need my rent in two weeks' time. Got it?"

Not wanting to provoke him any further, I just nod. A sigh of relief builds up when he goes to leave, but gets stuck in my chest when he turns back again with a wicked grin on his face.

"Nice security system by the way. Would be a shame if something were to happen to pretty girls like you."

Something creepy crawls up my spine as he looks us both up and down. I swallow the disgust and pick up my roller again, ready to whack him in the face.

"What's going on here?"

Stella and I bump into each other as we jump at the voice behind us. I am shocked by Max's sudden appearance. We didn't even hear him come in. It's like watching a movie when he crosses us to get into Frank's face. Not that he has to, Frank is a short man. The top of his head doesn't even reach Max's chest. A second later, Frank moves back, ending the glaring contest.

"Two weeks," he points a pudgy finger at me before leaving.

When the door slams behind him, rattling the windows, I take out a chair and plop down onto it, burying my head into my hands. A hand rubs at my back.

"It'll be okay, Lil," Stella tries to calm me down.

When? I ask myself. When will it all be okay? And how? I don't see anything changing in the near future. If it does, I'm sure it'll only get worse. The chair across me is pulled out, Max's knees bump into mine as he takes a seat.

"Lily, can we talk about it now?"

I lower my hands to look at him through the tears in my eyes.

"Talk about what?"

He glances behind me at Stella then looks at me again.

"About me being a partner?"

I immediately shake my head. He throws his hands up.

"Hear me out, Lily. Let me help you, financially at least!"

"Max, I appreciate you. I really do," I repeat when he narrows his eyes at me. "But I do not want your money."

"Setting up a restaurant with you won't even make a dent in my inheritance. You need to reconsider," he says while standing up. "And soon, by the looks of it."

The windows rattle once again as he slams the door too. Silence descends in the shop until Stella speaks.

"Have you considered installing a pneumatic door closer?"

I laugh in spite of myself before getting to my feet and continuing painting again.

***

With all the arrangements made for the bake sale, I finally start hearing about it on the streets. Mom was the one who took the council's permission to use the space in front of the clock tower in question. It is the central landmark of Hillgrove and I've never seen it work in the two years I've been here. My family and Stella's have been distributing pamphlets all day. They even drove around town to slip it beneath people's doors. In the meanwhile, I shopped for groceries for tomorrow.

Now that I'm heading back home, I find people holding the pamphlets, discussing and whispering about. A part of me wants to slow down and listen to what they have to say. But it is smaller than the other part that is telling me to pedal harder.

I stop at the bookstore on the way back. Mr. Williams looks up as the bell on the door announces my arrival. I smile as he perks up when he sees it's me.

"Lily! Where have you been, kid?"

I shrug, not having the words to explain. But I know he knows either way. Nothing in this town is ever a secret. I take out a pamphlet from my bag and hand it to him. He instantly lowers his glasses and starts reading.

"It's for the clock tower," I explain though it is mentioned.

"This is brilliant!" He exclaims after a moment of reading, and I let out the breath I was holding.

"Do you think it will work?"

"Even if it doesn't, I think it's bloody amazing of you to be willing to fight and prove them wrong."

I look to the side as heat rises to my face at his compliment. It doesn't occur to me what I'm looking at, until the very second I'm about to look away. It's the book, the very same book, I saw at Cora's. I walk to his desk and pick it up.

"Mr. Williams, where did this book come from?"

He pulls up his glasses to look at it from so far away, while my heart gallops in my chest.

"Cora returned it just today. It is part of the library, you see."

I open it, and sure enough, there is a record slip at the back. Countless names are listed on it. Cora's being the latest. The book wasn't hers after all. I look at the list of names again. Hannah's name stands out. She borrowed it a whole year ago. I put it back down.

"I'll see you tomorrow?"

He gives me a smile and a thumbs up, "Definitely."

***

While I'm unpacking the groceries in the kitchen, my phone rings. I pick it up without checking the screen.

"Hello?"

"What part of keeping a low profile did you not understand?" Sadie gets straight to the point as always.

"You didn't tell me to keep a low profile. You told me to stick to my usual routine," I remind her.

"So jog up my memory please, because I can't remember a single time your usual routine included a bake sale for the whole town."

"Sadie there's someone out there trying to frame me for a murder of a person I cared about. Tomorrow is the best chance they'll get to sabotage me. So if you're really worried about me, worry about how to catch them when they do."

I check the screen to check if the call is still going on when she stays silent for a while before speaking again.

"I'll set my eyes on the ground. It is indeed a good setting for the killer to slip up. But I still want you to be as careful as you possibly can. Only let the people you trust with your life to look over your products. We don't need another frame job on our hands."

"Thanks Sadie. I'll be vigilant."

Chapter 11

Chapter 11

I rush inside once all the boxes are loaded up in Dad's truck. Loki follows me around, on edge because of everyone scuttering around my house. I scoop him up into my arms while refilling his food bowl. Luke takes the packet from me and does it. When he is done, he gestures to take Loki. I hand him the anxious cat, knowing they both calm each other down.

"What else is there?" Dad asks, walking back in with Mom.

Max and Polly follow them in too. I asked Stella to sleep in, knowing Hazel kept her up all night. She's already in the loop and knows what I'm about to tell everyone else. Sadie told me to only keep the ones I trust with me. So here they are.

"I have to tell you all something."

They gather around the kitchen counter. Luke comes to stand beside me. With all of them looking at me so attentively, this moment feels bigger than it is.

"I have a feeling that whoever killed Marco, will attempt something again today."

They all suck in a breath and anxiously look at each other.

"I don't want you all to be worried. I just want you to be alert. If something seems off, tell me. There will be police all around us, they will help. Okay?"

Sounds of agreement echo as they all nod and relax at the mention of law enforcement being present.

"Oh my look at the time, Lily go get dressed!" Mom urges me into my bedroom with a hand on my back.

I flip a few hangers but have trouble deciding. Clothes are my thing. I never have a problem putting a killer outfit together. But what does one even wear on a day such as this? I take out a dress. Nope, too formal. I hang it back and take out a skirt.

"Can't decide what to wear?"

I turn to look at Polly standing in the doorway.

"Wanting to present the best version of myself while also looking laidback is the goal," I hold up the two hangers in my hands. "No pressure, right?"

She smiles and walks over. I notice she is wearing something I would've worn on any other day. Her silk skirt is long enough to be modest but short enough to show the stockings and a peek of garter underneath. Her sleeveless sweater vest is paired with a white button-up. Judging by the lack of visible lines in the skirt, I'm guessing it's a crop top.

"Nice outfit girl," I grin at her.

She flushes, and waves a hand in the air. "It's nothing."

"One second," Curiosity gets the best of me and I step closer to her, plucking her sweater away from her skirt. My hand brushes bare skin and I nod to myself, *crop top indeed*. She gasps and forcefully grabs my hand.

I step back instantly, "I'm sorry—"

"No, your hands are just really cold," she caresses my wrist she'd been gripping before letting it go.

"Sorry," I wince and back up, holding up the hangers again. "So?"

She looks between the two options, a finger on her chin.

"Wear the cream trousers and vest."

I hang the skirt back and take out the matching shirt. She stops me, and puts it back.

"Lose the shirt. Make them stare," she winks and leaves.

I tilt my head at the vest. It does make a statement.

"Fair enough."

***

People are indeed staring. But not at me. No, they're staring at the sweet, baked goods in front of me.

I sold three trays of brownies in the first hour. It was a sight to see. Mr. Williams and Donald were my first customers. Seeing them buying from me, a few more older people joined in and bought cookies. Once they left, friends of my parents showed up. All of them are respected fellows of the community. Their example was followed by many people crossing the street.

Mom left earlier with Luke. It's just me, Dad, Polly, and Max now. I hang back once I see people are on edge because of me. They start pooling at the table again and we make more sales. I handle the payments until Polly takes a seat beside me.

"Tired?" I ask her while handing her a juice box as she stretches her legs out in front of her.

"No offense, but this is harder than I expected it to be."

"To be very honest, it's going better than I expected."

"People miss your desserts," she says, scratching her palm.

"You can go home and rest. You've done more than enough."

"Are you sure?"

I nod, "Thanks a lot for today."

She smiles and squeezes my shoulder. "Any time."

When she leaves, I poke my finger on Dad's shoulder. He turns to look at me.

"Go have lunch, Dad. You can come back later if you want."

"I'm good," he shrugs, "not that hungry right now."

I turn to Max, "It's time for your brunch."

He chuckles, "It definitely is. I'll bring you guys sandwiches from Rina's. Want anything else?"

Dad tells him his preference and he leaves too. Dad nudges me once he's gone.

"Good boy, isn't he?"

I huff, "He is. He is also *only* my friend."

Dad raises his hands up in the air, playing the innocent. "I didn't say anything."

"I know what you meant."

"What's that?"

"I'm happy to be on my own, Dad. At least for another year."

Pulling me into him by the shoulders, he kisses my forehead. "I just don't want you to be lonely, muffin."

"I'm not."

"Good."

A group arrives at the table. I look up to see a few members of the council. Tom's aunt stands to the side with a scowl on her face, next to a woman with a mirroring scowl. The men all smile as they make small talk with Dad and place their orders. I hand them the change.

"And what would the ladies like?" Dad asks the scowling women with a huge smile on his face.

"I have no intention to be poisoned today, James," Tom's aunt says, still scowling.

"Some other day then," Dad replies without missing a beat.

I bite my lip to hide my smile, while one of the men coughs. Her face reddens as she glares at us before stomping away with the other woman.

"It's a good thing you're doing, Lily," the man in the middle says to me. "We appreciate it. Well, some of us do."

With that, they all walk away. I turn to my father.

"You're awesome, Dad."

He just beams at me and takes a seat behind the table. I restock the trays on the table and cover them again. Then duck down to count the empty trays. I am amazed when I see that all the trays beneath the table are empty. That means only one tray of brownies and one tray of cookies are left.

"Dad?"

"Yes?"

"Did we really sell all of our cupcakes?"

"All twenty of them," he grins.

"Should I go bake more?"

"If you want to," he shrugs. "It *is* for a good cause. But you're not keeping any of it, are you?"

"No, I'm not."

"It is up to you then."

I'm thinking it over when a shadow falls over the table. I look up, surprised to see Detective Roberts standing on the other side. Dressed in black like always, I wonder how he is not sweating bullets in the sun.

"Hello Dr. Grayson," he nods at my father, then looks at me. "Miss Grayson."

"Aiden!" Dad stands up and gives the man a hearty handshake.

I look between them in confusion. *They know each other?*

"How have you been?" Dad asks, "Any trouble with the knee?"

The detective gives him a small, polite smile. "I'm good, thanks to you."

"Oh no, it was all you. Still keeping up the exercise?"

"As much as I can."

"Good, then you won't have any qualms about buying a brownie or two."

I'm as lost as a helium balloon without a string when they both turn to me. Dad pats my shoulder to bring me forward just as his phone rings. He excuses himself and steps aside to take the call. Still frowning at the black haired man who is looking at me without even the small smile he eagerly gave my father, I step ahead.

"What can I get you?"

"I was hoping for banana bread."

I search for a sign that he's joking but don't find a single one. For some reason, it frustrates me to no end. I cross my arms and tip my chin up.

"I only make that for special people. You can have a brownie."

He ducks his head to look at his options.

"I'll take this lot," he points at the ones with almonds.

I automatically pick up a bag for one, and stop.

"The *lot*?"

"Yeah, the tray, all of it."

Is he mad? I love brownies, but even I don't eat a whole tray in a day. Where does he even put them? I wonder as I take a look at his impressive physique. My dad's return pulls me out of it. I get to work. Thankfully, I brought boxes to pack up the leftovers. Since I will not be having any leftovers, I pack up the brownies in a box and hand it to him. I take his money and hand him the change. He takes it but his eyes search for something around the table. Instantly on guard, I look around too.

"What's wrong?" I ask when I don't see anything fishy.

"Where's the tip jar?"

I halt my search and look up at him. His brows are knitted close together over his stunning eyes. He looks visibly confused, and also adorable.

Dad jumps in to answer, "All the proceeds will go to the council for the clock tower's reparation."

"Okay," he nods, still frowning.

I think about it. The thought of a tip jar didn't even occur to me today.

"Have a nice day, Aiden," Dad says and he nods at him before leaving with the box of my last brownies.

My mind is still reeling over the last few minutes when Max returns with our food. I wait for Dad to come back before opening my sandwich. We both eat while Max handles the last sales. I'm throwing away my wrapper when I see Hannah walking up the street.

"Hey Max, can you pack everything up? I'll be back in a minute."

I run to catch up to her, and slow down when I'm close.

"Hannah?"

She turns around, and stops to wait when she sees it's me.

"Hi. Need any help?" I gesture at the grocery bags in her hands.

"Thank you," she hands me one and we resume walking.

I've been to their place a couple of times and I know that it is not too far from here. So I need to be quick.

"How are you?"

She shrugs. I nod, understanding her all too well.

"Having a hobby helps. For me it's baking. Whenever I feel overwhelmed, I bake."

"I meditate. It calms me down."

"Are you into gardening too?"

She falters. My heart does too.

"No. Why?"

"No reason," I take a breath to calm my shaky voice. "I thought meditating worked well in a garden."

"I keep a few plants with me. Nothing much."

"Do you know where I can read up on plants? I was thinking of sprucing up my place a bit."

"Polly could answer that question better than I can. You should ask her."

Not knowing what more to say without being too direct, I drop it. When we turn into her street, she turns to take the bag from me.

"I once borrowed a book from Mr. Williams's library for Polly. She said it was a great help for her. Maybe you'd like it too? I can have it sent to your house, if you want?"

Staring at her, I realize that I am barking up the wrong tree. She really has no interest in gardening.

"Thank you, but I'll take a look at the library the next time I go there."

She smiles at me, and lifts up the bag, "Thank you for this. Have a great day."

I give her a small wave and walk back to our table. Dad already has everything loaded up on the back of his truck by the time I get back. Max hands me the bag with all the empty containers.

"I'm heading back home. Do you need something?"

I pretend to think about it, tapping a finger on my chin.

"Come to think of it, I do."

"What is it?"

"A hug."

I smile as he rolls his eyes and bends down to hug me.

"Thank you," my voice is muffled into his shirt.

When he backs up and leaves, I walk to Dad's truck. It is warm and smells like Dad's aftershave. I relax into the seat.

Dad hands me the envelope containing the money. I smile at him. He leans over the console and hugs me.

"Congratulations kiddo, it was a success."

"Thanks for being here, Dad."

He ruffles my hair and starts the car.

"I'm taking you home with me. Your mom's calling you for dinner."

"Can we drop off the money at the council's first?"

"Sure."

***

When we reach home, Mom is waiting there at the entrance with Luke at her side. We walk up the driveway and Luke brandishes a party popper from his back when we're close enough. Pop it goes. I laugh as the confetti floats in the air around us. Mom hugs me, swaying us from side to side.

"I'm so proud of you, my sweet girl."

I kiss her cheek and lean down to hug Luke. It is disarming how little I have to, since he is almost up to my shoulders now.

Spending time with my family always fills me with peace. After the day I had, I feel better about my whole situation already. No matter what comes tomorrow, I know that I tried my best to salvage my standing in this town.

My phone rings and I send them all in when I see that it's Sadie.

"Hi Sadie."

"Hey," She sounds relaxed for a change. "How did it go?"

"I just handed over five thousand dollars to the council. So I'd say pretty well."

"That's amazing, Lily. Good for you."

"Thanks. So did you guys notice something off?"

I hear her sigh over the phone.

"I'm sorry to be the one to say this Lily, but there's a high chance that the killer is someone from your circle."

"What?" I frown. "Why would you say that?"

"Because they're the only ones who knew that you were counting on the killer to mess up and that the police were there. No one else knew. They were all undercover."

"No, Sadie. It's impossible. I trust them all. There's no way what you're saying applies to them."

"For your sake, I hope not. Enjoy your win, Lily."

"Sadie," I rub my forehead, "I— What about Frank?"

"He's come out clean so far. We're still working on him. The toxicologist is narrowing down poisons too. It's all in process. I'll tell you when there's an update. Until then, I want you to relax."

I sigh, "Okay."

I fall back against the wall when she hangs up. *What did I ever do for karma to mess me up so bad?*

Chapter 12

Chapter 12

I wake up feeling not too different as I did yesterday. My big 3-0 is overshadowed by a feeling of doubt and unease. I hardly feel like myself these days.

At twenty, I had imagined thirty-year-old Lily as a happy mother of two, living in a beach house with a white picket fence and a garden blooming with cute little jasmines. I had imagined all of that along with a restaurant I would work at during second shifts while my husband looked after our kids.

Then I got divorced at twenty-four. So, on my twenty-fifth birthday, I'd been all for being an independent woman at thirty. I had imagined myself with a hefty bank balance, owning a restaurant I would work at all day, and waking up everyday with a smile on my face because I didn't have another person I needed to pick up after.

Now at thirty, I am bankrupt and I certainly haven't woken up with a smile on my face in months. As if he can hear my thoughts, Loki jumps on the bed and curls up on the pillow next to me. I pet him for a while before my alarm starts blaring.

It is still dark out when I leave earlier than usual today to see the sunrise from the hill just past the forest. I switch between jogging and walking, conserving my energy for the climb. Just as I start moving, my mind is flooded with thoughts about Marco's murder. All the clues, questions, leads packed into a jumbled pattern.

I close my eyes and take a deep breath to clear my mind. Save all the thinking for the top of the hill, I tell myself.

I reach the hill and stop at the base. As much as I love running, I really don't like doing it on an incline. But the view from this hill is worth it. I leave a text to Stella to find my body here in case I die of exhaustion. That is if she doesn't die first. Hazel was sick all day yesterday. After forty-eight hours of running on fumes to tend to her daughter, Stella only fell asleep two hours ago.

Motivating myself, I start climbing. The slow ascension kills my lungs. I stop somewhere in the middle, bent at the waist with my hands on my knees, but the sky's change in color catapults me into motion again. Sweat drips down my hairline and neck. I take off my hoodie from over my tank top and wrap it around my waist.

The first strand of orange sneaks out of the horizon. I keep one eye on the sky and one on the path ahead of me. I'm almost there. My thighs burn and my fingers do too with the need to itch at my legs. I am huffing and puffing by the time I reach the top. I nearly fall to the ground in relief, only to stop in my tracks as I spot someone at my bench.

Not that it is my bench, I only come here like once a year, but it was where I was going to sit and watch the sun rise.

I take a step back, thinking of finding another place. Then step ahead again, I didn't climb up all this way for nothing! But what if he's a pervert?

"I can hear your thoughts from up here, Miss Grayson."

To say I am shocked would be an understatement. Detective Roberts is the last person I expected to find here at this ungodly hour. Once I get over my shock of seeing him here, my mind goes numb over his matching black t-shirt and shorts. Good to know that he looks handsome both in and out of a suit.

I do my best to appear unfazed by the hike and walk up to the edge where he is.

"How did you even know it's me up here? Are you following me?"

"Anyone could've heard your hyperventilation from a mile away."

My jaw drops, "Wow, you didn't have to diss me like that."

He huffs out a chuckle. "You made it to the top, didn't you?"

"I did. So if you don't mind, I'd like to enjoy the sunrise in peace."

Instead of getting the hint and leaving, he crosses his arms and gets comfier, stretching his crossed legs in front of him.

"Be my guest," he shrugs, looking straight ahead at the horizon.

My eyes roll in annoyance as I give up and take a seat next to him. The sky has taken a beautiful hue as the orange mixes in with the blue. The birds haven't yet woken up. In the silence, thoughts I'd been holding at bay threaten to overcome my mind again. The view of Hillgrove peacefully sleeping while holding my sanity captive bothers me. I think about what my future looks like in this town if Marco's real killer isn't apprehended, and if it's even worth the fight. I had multiple job offers in Paris. I still have good contacts. I could go back there. Though I know I could never leave with this question unanswered. I have always been a curious person. But this goes deeper than mere curiosity.

"Detective, tell me something."

"Hmm?" He turns to me, broken out of his own musings.

"Do you think Marco knew who killed him?"

His head tilts to the side as he looks at me with piqued interest.

"It's highly possible. Since he died of poisoning, he must have known who gave it to him."

"Could he have left a clue for us— I mean, the police?"

He shakes his head, "We thoroughly searched the alley we found him in. There was nothing of the sort."

Disappointed again, I cross my arms and lean back. The muted orange in the sky has grown but the sun is nowhere to be seen.

"Miss Grayson?"

I look at him and notice that he looks quite boyish with his uncombed hair falling onto his forehead.

"Yes?"

"Do you enjoy living in Hillgrove?"

My heart goes still for a second as he hits the nail right on the head before resuming with a gallop, making me cough all of a sudden. A laugh sputters out of me when I'm finally able to take a breath.

"Can you really hear my thoughts?"

He smiles, "It would make my job a lot easier if I could indeed hear everyone's thoughts."

"You wouldn't be a very good detective then, would you?"

"No, I wouldn't."

I look away from the crinkle of his eyes towards the visible curve of the glowing ball of light.

"Do *you* enjoy living in Hillgrove?"

"Poor form Miss Grayson," there's a teasing lilt to his tone as he clicks his tongue.

"Learn to give before you take, detective."

He huffs out a silent laugh, his dimple winking through his stubble. Then rubs his jaw, thinking about it. I can't tear my eyes away from him even after he answers.

"It has its ups and downs."

"Do you think you'll still have a good life here if you fail to solve this case?"

I bite my lip waiting for his answer, hoping he doesn't realize that all my insecurities underline the innocent question.

"I can, if I get to keep my job and don't care what other people think of me."

Both things I can't do. I sigh and lean back against the bench, wrapping my arms around myself. After a moment, he breaks the silence.

"But I won't fail."

I look at him again. "How are you so sure?"

"Because I have great partners."

I hold myself back from gushing over how smart and professional Sadie is to not raise his suspicion of knowing her too well.

"Yeah," I nod in agreement, "you do have that."

The sun is now a golden dome over the skyline. Hillgrove is awake too. I can just make out a few people moving about on the running track in the park. It is mainly the reason why I don't go there for my morning run. Early morning socializing is not really my forte.

"Ready to give back?" he reminds me of my earlier words.

I smirk, wanting to tease him a bit. "It has its ups and downs."

He narrows his brilliant eyes and shakes his head at me. I chuckle at his mock annoyance.

"No really, I like living here. Where else would I get to see such a beautiful sunrise?" I gesture at the view in front of us.

"And do you like the people of Hillgrove?"

I don't know why I keep forgetting how intuitive he is. The pale sunlight catches his eyes, elevating them to look otherworldly. Feeling cold all of a sudden as goosebumps erupt on my bare skin, I untie my hoodie from my waist and put it on.

"I like them when they're not judging me for things I didn't do."

He nods, and turns back to the sunrise. I do too. The sun, though weak, is out and has lit up the sky. The sound of cars interferes with the melodious chirping of birds. It reminds me of the beautiful day yesterday.

"Do you mind if I ask you a question?"

He raises an eyebrow at me, as if to say, *now you're asking?* I roll my eyes, unable to hold off the smile spreading over my face.

"What happened to your knee?"

Unconsciously the leg in question twitches beneath the other one. He crossed them when I arrived and hasn't moved since. I guessed it's because he has a scar from the surgery he must have had, since my dad was his doctor. What I would've never guessed is for him to be conscious about it.

"I was shot."

His reply isn't curt, but I get the unmistakable feeling that he is uncomfortable with telling me more. So, before the silence gets to him, I say the first thing that pops into my head.

"Are you free tonight?"

I suck in and hold my breath as he looks at me with surprise coloring his features. Not sure I'm faring any different. I'm shocked by myself too.

"I mean, for—"

"I don't think—"

We speak over each other, causing me to snap my mouth shut while he does the same. I know what he was about to say. I don't think that's a good idea. It's written all over his face. I can't believe how easily I ruined the excellent start to my day. I shoot to my feet, my eyes on the ground.

"Excuse me, umm... goodbye."

Not waiting around for his reply, I cross the bench quickly and sprint away, tripping on a rock a few feet from the bench. I check over my shoulder and thank heavens that he's still facing the other way.

Good lord, why do I always make a fool of myself around this man?

***

My phone rings with yet another call. Thinking that it is Mom to remind me of the time again, I let it ring. When it starts ringing again, I put down the hot curler away from Loki and pick up my phone.

"Hello?"

"Lily I've got good news and bad news," Sadie jumps straight into it.

"Let's hear them."

"Good news first. The toxicologist narrowed down the poison. Why don't you visit me at the station tomorrow? We'll talk more about it there."

"You sure about that?"

"Yeah. For the bad news," she sighs. "Frank has thrown you under the bus. He brought in documents of your deal with Marco. Did you pay him less than what was stated?"

I pinch the bridge of my nose. This was supposed to be between me and Marco.

"Yes."

"Why?"

"It's a long story, but Marco wanted to do something good, something meaningful," I add, hoping she gets how important this is to me. "He asked me to pay it forward someday and I fully intend to. It was a promise between us. How does Frank know about it?"

"I don't know. But Lily, do you have it in writing? Your word means nothing until it is on paper of some sort."

I halt as déjà vu hits me full force. I cannot believe Marco's good gesture is coming back around in a form much similar to my worst experience of divorcing my husband. Where not a single claim of mine had been held true in court just because I had been stupid enough to trust a gambler's son and had let him handle my finances. Even though I had promised myself to not repeat the same financial mistakes, I went and did it again. So now, I have no one to blame but myself.

"No," I solemnly admit. "I don't."

Chapter 13

Chapter 13

My knife cuts through the cake that I didn't bake as everyone sings me a 'Happy birthday'. While blowing out the candles, I only had one wish; for this nightmare to be over soon.

"Happy birthday, sweetheart," Mom kisses me on the cheek and feeds me a spoonful of cake.

I thank her and hand over the knife to her. Luke helps her with handing everyone a slice, giving me the chance to slip away for a much needed breather. I hardly know anyone at this party; most of the attendees being my parents' colleagues and their families. They are the only ones who are old and isolated enough to not care about what goes on in the town. Because of all the senior citizens in attendance, it is more a gala than a birthday dinner.

Drinks refilled, I lean against the wall to look at everyone in the hall. Mr. Williams looks right at home in the crowd, laughing with two other elderly men. I find Max on the other side of the room, cornered by a group of women. His charming smile is in place until he catches sight of me. He gives me his best pleading look to make me save him but I just smile and shake my head. If I can go through my mom introducing me to single men all night, so can he. Ryan, Stella's husband, is sat with Hannah and her nephew, who is also friends with Luke.

"Oh god, please tell me that is something non-alcoholic."

I lean over the mini-fridge and pull out a fruit soda for Stella. She went to breastfeed her daughter in my old room, wanting some quiet as Hazel usually goes to sleep after being fed.

"Hazel's asleep?" I ask her as she gulps down the drink.

"Finally."

I smile at the relief in her tone and take another sip of my wine.

"By the way bamboo," she waves a hand towards my body, "where did you get your outfit from?"

It is a burgundy knitwear fitted dress. Well, it used to be. Now it is a skirt and an off-shoulder top that shows off my figure quite nicely. My shoulder rises as I coquettishly bat my lashes at her.

"This old thing?"

She laughs at my antics. "There's nothing old about this. I haven't seen it on you before."

"It was a dress when I bought it from the mall. But the waist was all wrong. So I cut the middle part and sewed this lace on the skirt and top to give it a finished look."

Stella grins at me in awe, but before she can say anything, I am startled by someone's hand on the exposed part of my waist.

"And what a great idea that was," Polly grins from my side. "You look phenomenal, hun."

I relax when I see it's her, yet inconspicuously adjust us both so her hand isn't on my skin.

"Thanks. Have you had cake?"

"I'm about to. Your mom's calling you."

"I'll be right there," I sigh.

When Polly leaves with a kiss on the bottom of my jaw, not being too tall to reach my cheek, I turn to Stella. She stands next to me with a deep frown on her face. I can feel her breathing.

"What?"

"I forgot how much she's…" she shudders and takes my glass of wine, gulping it down.

I nudge her middle with my elbow.

"Be nice."

"I am! Didn't I tell you to make nice with her? But why is she so handsy? You're not even that comfortable with her."

"I'll get there. But I'm not going to stop her from expressing herself."

"Do you think she's bi?" she whispers, wary of the people around us.

"So what if she is?" I shrug.

"Why hide?"

"She just got divorced. She can't exactly shout it from the rooftops and risk getting slandered by the whole town."

"I think she's into you in a twisted way. Just like him," she rolls her eyes as she sees someone behind me.

I turn around to look at whoever is there, and am not surprised to see Max. Though I will never understand what the beef between them both is, I'm still no stranger to it. Stella is a really good judge of character so I always heed her warnings, but her reservations with Max are a little too much.

"Thanks for helping me back there," Max says sarcastically.

I laugh but stop at Stella's reply.

"It didn't look like you were minding all the attention."

"Couldn't exactly have told the ladies that I wasn't enjoying their company," Max says with his lips pressed into a thin smile. "Unlike some people, I'm good mannered, you see."

With another scoff and eye-roll, Stella turns to pick up another soda. Max looks at me.

"Happy birthday," he leans down to softly kiss my cheek.

"Thank you."

He straightens up and takes an envelope out of his pocket.

"This is for you."

Curious, I take the envelope from him. A metallic object sits in the corner. I turn the envelope upside down and catch it in my hand. Frowning, I look up at Max.

"It's a car key," I state as a matter of fact.

"It's your car key."

"I don't understand."

Stella comes to stand beside me as I stare at Max, dumbfounded by the key in my hand.

"I bought back your jeep. It's yours again," Max grins at me.

My jeep. My jeep! He bought me back my jeep. I clutch the key as I hug him tightly.

"Max, I—" Words escape me as I release him. "Thank you—"

"Hey, Mr. Good mannered," Stella hands Max my empty wine glass, "get her a refill please."

I am taken back by her sudden interjection. Max glares at her but still takes the glass and stomps towards the kitchen.

I turn to Stella, "What the hell was that about, Stel?"

"Your jeep? Seriously?"

"I know! I can't believe he would do something like this."

She rolls her eyes, "Sure he would."

"What do you mean by that?"

"Lily, the guy has been pining over you for the last three years. He even followed you to this dumb little town."

"He's not pining—"

"Need I remind you of the time he didn't talk to his landlord just so you could keep living at his place in Paris?"

I shake my head, knowing where this is going since we've had this conversation a million times before.

"Max is a friendly person, Stella. He was trying to help me then, and he's only trying to help me now."

"If he was really trying to help you then he wouldn't have thrown it in your face the first chance he got."

"Sometimes I really regret telling you every single thing."

She chuckles but quickly schools her smile, "He'll just do the same thing again. He'll always want to have the upper-hand if he can't have you. That's just the kind of person he is."

I twist the key in my hand. It slowly occurs to me how quickly I jumped the gun again. He bought me a freaking car! That can't be any good on paper.

Before I can reply, we are joined by others.

"Honey, I've been looking for you all over the place," Mom gently tugs at my arm.

I am faced with yet another unknown man. He seems kind enough with the polite smile on his face, but his eyes wander from my face all the way down to my toes.

"Lily, meet Harry. Harry," she gestures between us with a wide smile on her face. "Lily."

Harry, to my surprise, forgoes the standard handshake and leans in to blow kisses against both my cheeks. Behind him, I see Stella press her lips together to hide her grin.

"Nice to meet you, Lily. You're just as beautiful as your mother said you are."

I glare at Mom, who just shrugs innocently.

"What else did she say?"

Harry glances apprehensively between us all for a split second before his smile widens again.

"Nothing she said, but I did hear that you're smack in the middle of a murder case. How interesting! Are you allowed to talk about it?"

I grit my teeth. "No, I'm not. Excuse me."

I hear Mom's sigh as I walk by her to find Max. I don't understand why she can't just leave me to my devices. Dad was just asking me about it yesterday. Is it really even that big of an issue? They didn't seem to approve when I got married at nineteen. And they don't seem to approve now. Will I ever truly make my parents hap—

"Are you crazy?"

I stop near the kitchen as I hear Max's loud voice from inside.

"She came onto me!"

Who did? I want to ask, but I keep quiet and stay out of sight.

"I am not crazy," a woman replies in a low, calm voice. "But if you speak about this to anyone, I'll happily show you what crazy is."

I realize that it is Polly in there with him. Too confused, I warily peek inside, just in time to see Polly backing away from Max, putting something in her pocket. He stares at her wide-eyed, still against the wall. I wait around the corner to see everything unfold, but am distracted by a shadow escaping to the backyard where Dad's car is. Following a whim, I quickly take the hallway to follow the person sneaking out. *Could it be the killer?* I pick up speed and the figure comes into view. They're scurrying away, nearly at the gate. In the faint light, I notice that it's a woman.

"Hey! Stop!"

Making the chase, I catch up to her and stop her by the arm.

"Wha—Oh."

I pause when I see it's Hannah. And she's crying.

"Hannah what happened?"

She sobs, unable to speak, and smothers herself into me. Her tears wet my neck. I shush her, rubbing her trembling back.

"Whatever it is, it'll be okay. You'll be fine."

After a minute of consolation, she finally straightens up, wiping her face with the back of her hands.

"I'm so s-sorry Lily," her chin wobbles as she speaks. "I thought—but she— I can't. Marco…"

I fight back my own tears as she starts weeping again.

"It's okay if you want to leave early. Your nephew can sleep here."

She nods, "Thank you."

I wait outside the gate to make sure she is okay to drive. When her tail lights disappear, I lean back against the wall and let out an audible sigh, finally able to relax out of the public eye.

"Long day?"

I gasp and straighten up, startled by the unexpected voice. Detective Roberts, dressed in black like always, seems to appear out of thin air. Lights from the house illuminate only half of his face.

"What are you doing here?"

Hands in pockets, he just shrugs. Dread settles in my gut. I imagine he's here to question me about what Frank said. I stay quiet, knowing I can't be the first to say something since Sadie was the one who told me; and stay locked in a staring contest with the most disarming man I've ever met.

Finally he moves, taking something out of the inside pocket of his huge coat. He holds out a box wrapped in brown paper. It looks rather like a book.

"Is that a gift?" I ask as I take it from him.

"It's a token."

"Of?"

My fingers pick at the wrapper while I wait for his answer. His head lowers as he looks at the ground. My gaze follows, but I find nothing to keep my attention. It's definitely a book, I realize as I feel it in my hands. I could find a book anywhere with my eyes closed. When I look back up, his eyes are intently focused on mine.

"Of acknowledgement."

My head tilts as I try to discern his meaning, but his next words only confuse me more.

"I know more than you think I do, Miss Grayson. I'm starting to realize that you do too. This," he nods towards the book in my hands, "is me acknowledging that."

"You're not coming inside?" I ask as he steps away.

"I have some work to do." His eyes twinkle as he smirks, "Happy birthday, Miss Grayson. Have fun."

I smile, sensing the sarcasm in his tone. He knows fun is the last thing on my mind. I watch him walk away until he turns the corner. As soon as he is gone, I carefully unwrap the book in my hand. 'The Clue in the Diary' the title reads. Gaping, I look up to where he disappeared. He got me a Nancy Drew book. Even with the implications running wild in my head, I'm still grinning as I go back in.

Chapter 14

Chapter 14

Stopping my leg from bouncing up and down again, I glance at Luke to make sure he didn't notice. Today is his parent-teacher conference; one that he wanted *me* to attend instead of our parents. I'm sure I'm more nervous than he is. He's confident that he aced all of his classes. I, on the other hand, don't want anyone to say something regarding the whole murder debacle and overshadow his achievements. That was my biggest concern but he told me he doesn't care about that.

Sometimes I think he is wise beyond his years; definitely wiser than I was at his age. His brown eyes shine with knowledge as he observes everyone around us. I smile at him when he sees me watching. He gives me a gap-toothed smile in return.

The door opens and his teacher comes out with a couple and their child. After they leave, he checks his clipboard for the next name.

"Luke Grayson?"

We both stand up and follow the teacher inside. It is strange seeing the classroom empty and quiet.

"Good morning. How're you doing Luke? You're not Mrs. Grayson," the teacher smiles, looking between me and Luke in question.

His warmth and baritone voice immediately puts me at ease as we take a seat in front of his desk.

"I'm his sister," I reply as Luke signs.

The teacher raises his hand in the universal 'okay' sign, replying to Luke before speaking to me.

"My name is Zachary Smith. I'm Luke's English teacher. Since I'm not acquainted with you, I don't know how well informed you are about his schooling. So if we could start with a basic introduction, that would be great."

The unexpected start gives me pause. I try to narrow everything down in my mind so as to not waste his time.

"Nice to meet you, Mr. Smith. I'm L—"

"Sorry to interrupt, but please call me Zachary or Zach."

"Zach," I nod, "I'm Lily. Luke and I had a lot of catching up to do up until recently, so this is a surprise,"

I see Luke gazing at me from the corner of my eye so I turn to him. He gives me a smile and a nod to give me the much needed boost.

"But I know how much he loves English class, hates Math but still maintains a B grade in it. He could do without Science but really enjoys History."

Luke signs, "*You wouldn't have known about the significance of the clock tower without me and my love for history.*"

With a chuckle, I agree with him, "That's for sure. I knew it was an important landmark but I didn't know that it was centuries old and had such significance in the town. So thanks for that."

Realizing that we kind of started our own conversation and left the teacher alone, I turn back towards him. Zach is watching us both with a soft smile on his face.

"It is great to see that Luke has such a strong bond with his family. There's nothing much to discuss about his academic skills since Luke is a remarkable student. His record is pretty solid."

"I sense a 'however' in your sentence."

Zachary smiles at Luke, sharing a knowing look with him.

"*However,* he doesn't participate in class, nor does he have many friends."

"I don't think not having many friends is a problem. About class participation though,"

Luke gives me the most innocent face he can muster when I look at him. I soften my voice so he doesn't feel like I'm rebuking him.

"Not cool bro. You can't lie to me like that. I would've helped you."

He sighs and signs, "*That's why I didn't tell you. I didn't want to add to your plate.*"

The knowledge that my family is as affected as I am, is a punch to the gut.

I sign to him, "*We'll talk about this later.*"

Then turn to Zach. "We'll work on this. I'm sure he'll improve in no time."

Zach nods, smile still in place. "I second that. I'll be giving you the good news at the next conference."

"Thank you. Is there anything else?"

"Luke, you know the drill."

Luke tells me to stay and waves at his teacher before leaving the room. Zach opens a file and picks up his pen.

"I figure this is your first conference, since your parents are always the ones who come with him."

"Yes, it is. Not that they were busy, but Luke was the one who asked me to join him today."

"He holds you in high esteem."

My mind blanks for a second. It surprises me that Luke told his teacher about me.

"Well, that's unexpected," I shrug, a smile on my face.

"He does. I gave his class a task just last week to write about the person who inspires them the most and he wrote about you."

"I— uh—" I sputter, astounded in the best way possible.

"Would you like to read it?"

Immediately, I almost say yes, but then I realize that it is something private and if Luke wanted to show me then he would've shown it himself.

"If he'll show me."

Zach nods to himself, and writes something on his paper.

"That is all, Miss Grayson, I—"

"I'm sorry to interrupt," I echo his earlier words, "but please call me Lily."

He chuckles, his thick-rimmed glasses slipping as his nose wrinkles, "It's a pleasure to have met you Lily."

He stands up to shake my hand and I do the same.

"Likewise, Zach."

I find Luke waiting outside for me and give him a big hug for being my brother.

***

Sadie calls me to the precinct under the guise of questioning me about what Frank said. I cross my arms and sink into my coat. Sadie sits in front of me on the other side of the desk, currently wringing the hell out of her mesh stress ball.

"The last thing I need right now is Frank entangling me in a lawsuit I can't win. Sadie, please tell me what I can do to avoid it."

"Give him money."

My eyebrows shoot up my forehead. "You mean *bribe* him?"

She bristles as I whisper the word.

"No! I mean pay him the rent and whatever amount is left. That will shut him up."

I shake my head, chuckling derisively. "If that were possible, I'd have done it ages ago. I wanted nothing more than to pay Marco back."

"I'm sorry, Lily." Sadie slumps in her seat.

"It's alright."

We sit in silence again, both deep in our own thoughts. I lean back and rotate the chair. As the room revolves, my eyes fall on the corner table at the far side of the room. A plastic bag sits on it. But it isn't the plastic bag that catches my attention; it is the go-to cup inside it that does. I stop my chair, my feet firm on the ground.

"Sadie, what is that?"

Her eyes widen as they follow my pointing finger.

"Shit, I was supposed to leave that in storage."

"Why do you have my bakery's cup in a plastic bag?" I ask her again, even though a logical part of me already knows the answer. *It's the emotional side that needs to hear it from her.*

"It's the murder weapon of this case," she breaks it to me in a gentle voice.

I nod, "Wolfsbane right?"

"Yes."

"I read up on it. It has a severely bitter taste." I ask her what kept me up last night, "How did Marco not notice it?"

"Our team says that since there were signs of his tongue being burnt. My guess is that he chalked it up to that. Or maybe he was also given something sweet to eat. The poison would've been hard to detect.

"Hillgrove doesn't allow civilians to grow wolfsbane. How did they even get their hands on it?"

"Whoever it was, is very clever. She made sure not to leave behind any fingerprints in every sense of the word."

"Or *he*," I raise an eyebrow at her.

"Statistically speaking, women are more likely to be convicted than men in a homicidal poisoning case of another man."

Which takes me back to my cup. I have trouble wrapping my head around the fact that I made coffee with my own hands and served it to someone who used it to poison someone else.

"Can I see it?"

Sadie looks around in confusion, "It is confidential."

"It is from *my* bakery. I might see something you guys missed. She scratches the back of head, thinking to herself, until she sighs.

"Know what? Go ahead."

Green signal received, I pick up the plastic bag. The feeling of holding Marco's murder weapon in hand prompts the unbearable urge to drop everything and just cry. However, I control it and examine the cup closely.

The instant I turn it upside down, I freeze.

"What is it?" Sadie asks.

With my world standing still around me, I shake my head and lie to my friend.

"Nothing."

Chapter 15

Chapter 15

In the deafening silence, blood roars in my ears, leaving me with nothing but my doubtful thoughts. For the first time since I've known him, I am thankful for Max being perpetually unpunctual. In the heat of the moment, I texted him to meet me at the bakery as soon as I left the precinct.

I turn the cup in my hand, my finger immediately finding my initials at the bottom. I still remember the day I got the budget to get rid of Styrofoam cups and get custom-made cups for Cups & Cakes. It was six months after opening and it was also the day Max moved here from Paris. To commemorate the day, we exchanged cups with our initials on them; 'LG' for me, and 'MS' for Max.

It is completely understandable why no one at the police station noticed anything wrong with the cup in evidence. Coincidentally, 'MS' also stands for Marco Sanchez. Despite all my suspicions, I couldn't find it in me to throw my friend under the bus without questioning him on my own first.

This waiting time gave me time to breathe and think. So when the door opens, I am behind the freshly painted counter, casually arranging items on the shelf.

"What's up?" Max says while approaching me.

I put the bowl down and look at him; his eyes, his charming smile. *I'm wrong*, I tell myself. There should be a reasonable explanation for what I saw at the precinct.

"I was just about to rearrange the cupboards," I manage to speak through the tight smile on my face. "Thought you should be here for it."

He smiles, taking off his jacket. "Sure, I told you to call me if you needed any help."

"I thought it'd be better if you knew what is where for when we reopen."

He nods, "Since I'm here, you can leave the heavy lifting to me."

"Sure." I put down the stack of plates in my hand, and lean against the counter to observe him as he starts placing the dishes into the allotted places.

"Hey Max?"

"Yeah?"

"Your grandfather is a floriculturist, right?"

He turns to me, his eyebrows knitted close together and a confused smile on his face.

"He is. I'm surprised you remember that."

"I remember because you told me you used to spend your summers there until Paris."

He smiles to himself, continuing the work again.

"I did. I used to wait all year long for the time I'd get to spend with him."

"You almost became a floriculturist too, right?"

"Yeah, until I discovered baking."

I get to my feet before getting to the point.

"Max, where's your cup? I didn't find it in any of the cupboards."

"Uhh... about that," he scratches the back of his head. "I lost it a few weeks ago."

"How?"

"I took it home and had some guests over. The next morning, I couldn't find it."

I hold my breath, "Which guests?"

"That doesn't concern you, Lil," he says and gets back to arranging the supplies.

Offering a solemn prayer to everything that is holy, I slip in between him and the counter. His eyes widen in surprise but he doesn't move away from me.

"Lily?"

"Max," I crane my neck to look at him and speak softly, "It's important that you tell me."

I see his throat bob as he gulps before whispering, "It was a party. I don't exactly remember everyone who came."

Just as I feared. But at least now I know he had nothing to do with Marco's death. I'm frowning at his shirt, when he draws even closer than he already is.

"Speaking of parties, where did you run off to on your birthday?"

"Nowhere," I step out to freedom, then turn to face him. "I heard you and Polly got caught up in an altercation."

He scowls, "Who said that?"

"So it's true?"

"Obviously not. What would we even argue about? I don't know her that well."

I give him a nod and drop it. I can't risk frustrating him by barking up the wrong tree. With his back to me, he slams the first cupboard shut. A few moments pass, and I notice the dense clouds outside the window, realizing that I have to hurry.

"Can you tell me about wolfsbane?"

He immediately stops and drums his fingers on the countertop. I take a cautious step away from him before he faces me, frown still on his face.

"Why are you asking such questions?"

"I was just thinking," I paste a smile on my face. "You know how I get when I'm thinking. So humor me please."

He strokes his chin with his palm, thinking to himself.

"It's a plant with big, purple flowers. About yay high," he gestures mid-waist. "Though I don't think it is legal to grow it here."

"How come?"

"I might be wrong but as far as I can remember, it is poisonous and very dangerous to handle."

I take a minute to decide if I can trust him. Memories of him supporting me and having my back on multiple occasions assail my mind. I fill my lungs with them as I breathe in. I can't believe I suspected him of doing something so horrendous.

"Do you think if someone had it imported here, there would be records of it?"

He snaps his fingers as if an idea occurred to him.

"I can ask my grandfather. He used to have a very skilled book-keeper. I'm sure he would have an answer."

"Thanks, that would be great! Can you call him now?"

His smile dims, "Right now?"

"Yeah, if you don't mind. It's kind of urgent."

I sigh and shut my eyes as he excuses himself and goes outside to make the call.

Why is confronting someone so difficult?

Before I can muster another thought, something cold presses onto my mouth and a foul smell overtakes my senses as soon as I gasp in surprise.

I try to fight off the arms around me but fail as darkness descends upon my vision and my limbs fall limply to the side.

***

A healthy splash of ice cold water on my face jolts me back to consciousness. I sputter awake but as I move to wipe my face, I realize my hands and legs are tied down to the chair I'm sitting on. I struggle against the binds to no avail. My wet hair and shirt sticks to my skin making me squirm uncomfortably.

Forcing myself to stop panicking for a moment, I reduce my panting into quiet breaths. Then take a look around. I'm tied to a chair inside a shed of some sort. What stops me in my tracks is the tall, purple plant in front of me.

Wolfsbane.

I push against the ropes again. Desperation clouds my judgement, knowing the killer is nearby. Tears flow down my cheeks. The hurt of Max's betrayal punches holes in my heart. I never should've let my guard down. The mistake might cause me my life.

Another icy smack steals all the air from my lungs. I keep my head down, trying to wear off the shock.

"Finally!"

My head whips up in surprise at the voice. The red curls are all I see as the empty bucket clatters against the floor. Numbness clutches my nerves in an unforgiving grip, before relief cuts through. It wasn't Max. *Oh god, it wasn't Max!*

"I thought you'd never stop sputtering like a fish out of water," Cora cackles.

I can do nothing except stare at her as she flips her hair over her shoulder and takes a step towards me.

"Not so cocky now, are you?"

"Why did you bring me here?"

My voice is nothing but a hoarse whisper. But she hears me. I know she does because her eyes light up with an evil glint.

"I brought you here to show you, no— remind you that you're *nothing*! You thought that you could mess with me but I'll end you a thousand times before you can land a blow on me," she sneers in my face.

I can't believe it. It was her all along. My gut kept telling me that and I still decided to listen to Sadie. And now I might not make it out of here alive.

With a kick to my chair, that I feel in my teeth, she struts away, pausing in front of the plant.

"Who helped you? I know you didn't do it alone. You couldn't have. You're all feelings and no brain." She faces me once more, "Tell me before I cut it out of you. Who is your partner?"

I clench my jaw and square my shoulders. I might die here but I refuse to be a coward. I will never tell her about Sadie.

"You have some nerve. I'll tell you who my partner was when you're in handcuffs behind bars."

"For what?" She laughs. "Kidnapping a murderer? If anything, the police will have to thank me."

I frown, taken aback by her words. Is she seriously going to frame me for Marco's death?

"I'm sure you know personally how dangerous this plant is," she narrows her eyes at me. "Isn't that why you were shaking like a dry leaf in the wind when you saw it?"

"I'm sure you're no stranger to it as well. How did you get it here?"

"I didn't have to strive too hard you see," she spits out. "Since you were kind enough to drop it in my lap after you were done with it."

"*I* was done with it? You better watch your mouth! You can't pin Marco's death on me. The police will find the truth sooner or later and you *will* be punished!"

She stops in her tracks. I'm relieved my words got through to her. I need her scared so she messes up and gives me an opening to escape somehow. However, I quickly realize that fear is far from her orbit. She knows she has the upper hand right now and she intends to fully utilize it.

"I will kill or be killed before you can frame me for his death."

"*Frame* you?" I scoff. "How can you be *framed* for a crime you committed?"

She kicks the bucket hard enough to send it flying.

"I DIDN'T KILL HIM!"

I shake my head disbelievingly. I will not be making the mistake of trusting anyone again.

"You can shout all you want. It will not change the truth. You killed Marco. Poisoned him with that very plant. Broke several laws by bringing it here. And now you're trying to wash your hands off by killing me."

The more I speak, the more frantic she gets. Pacing the floor, her head in her hands, she looks so much like the Cora I knew back in high school; just a bully with no one on her side.

"You're not as clever as you think you are. My friends were coming to see me. They'll know I'm missing. So you can add kidnapping and attempted murder to the long list of crimes you're going to jail for, Miss Reynolds."

The blow comes out of nowhere. Something metallic strikes my head. My vision swims as the overbearing ringing in my ears threatens to blast my head off. I try to hold on but lose the battle against the pain.

For the second time, darkness wins over my consciousness.

Chapter 16

Chapter 16

When I come to again, there's a pounding ache beating on my head that wasn't there before. I feel something drip down from my head to my lap. I fathom I got splashed again. But when I slowly blink my eyes open, the first thing I see is the bright red blood on my lap. My heart skips a beat as I realize that I'm still tied to the chair and Cora is nowhere to be found. I shiver, losing my mind a little as I see my nails turn blue.

Laboring against the ties, I try to remember if I ever watched a tutorial on how to get out of a situation like this. I glance around the space for something sharp. But I see nothing except the damned plant. Cora must have cleared out the space before running away. It occurs to me that it's raining outside. *Storming*, actually. Thunder roars as the raindrops clamor against the steel roof of the shed.

Hyperventilating as the panic of being stranded invades all my rational thoughts, I fear that I will die here alone, without being able to say goodbye to my family. Tears stream down my face. I sob, my voice muffled by the loud storm outside. I prepare myself for the imminent failure and clear my throat, before yelling as loud as I can.

"HELP!"

The instant hammering in my head makes me whimper. But I refuse to give up like this. Thinking of Luke and my parents, I call for help again. When my head threatens to split in half, I think of Stella and how she'll murder me herself when she finds out that I didn't try. I yell again, willing my voice to rise above the storm.

I weep as the pain grows out of bounds; my ears ring, vision going blurry. I realize this is the end. If no one finds me in time, I would die of a concussion and blood loss. I would die without being able to tell Sadie that Cora is the real killer. I would die before Detective Roberts discovers that I'm innocent. The memory of that peaceful sunrise we watched together comes unbidden into my mind. I realize that the reason he unnerves me so much is because I like him. I like his eyes and his smile. I would die without telling him that.

I sit up straight. *The bucket!*

I look around, craning my neck to look behind me. There it is. I lift my weight up and lean forward to put my weight on the tips of my toes. I wobble as a wave of vertigo hits me. It takes everything in me to not topple head first into the ground. The second it is close enough, I drop my weight back into the chair. Breathing hard from the exertion, I nudge my elbow into the bucket to check if it is loud enough. When the sound echoes in the shed, I thank the heavens above. Taking a deep breath, I hit my elbow sideways into the bucket repeatedly, as hard as I can. The racket reverberates in my head and in the shed. A battle cry escapes my mouth, louder than all the ones before. When I collapse, I know I'm done.

"I tried..."

My cold limbs don't respond. Darkness dots my vision. My eyes fall shut, numbness taking over. A bang echoes in the space, but I can't find the energy to look up.

"Lily! Are you there?"

I will my tongue to move but it doesn't. I hear the familiar voice again, muttering a long string of curses I don't catch. I feel the chair move, my upper body swinging with it.

"Lily? Can you open your eyes for me?"

The voice is urgent but kind. The hands on the ropes are quick but gentle. I try my best to do as he says but every cell in my being fails me.

"Please Lily. Come on, I know you can do it. You're stronger than this."

A damp cloth presses the side of my head right over my wound. The pain pulls me out of it. I gasp but no air travels into my lungs.

"That's it Lil, breathe. I'm going to pick you up now."

The warning is the only reason I don't throw up. Needles prick every inch of my body the second he moves me.

"Aiden..." I whimper in pain as he hurries out of the wretched shed.

His hand cradles my head to his chest. "I'm so sorry baby. Just hold on a little longer."

I hear Sadie's voice over his intercom, calling for an ambulance to his location. I don't have to wonder for long how she knows where we are because once we reach the mouth of the alley, I hear her voice and we're instantly sheltered against the onslaught of rain

"Shit! Is she conscious?"

"In and out. Ambulance ETA?"

"Less than a minute. I already called them but I wasn't sure of the location..."

I try to hold on like Aiden said, but her words blur into each other as her voice fades somewhere far away from me.

***

I open my eyes and instantly flinch at the bright lights, slowly blinking them open again. The white tiled ceiling of the hospital room addles my brain.

"Hey hun."

My mother comes into sight, standing at the side of my bed. She is wearing the same sad smile I saw on her face the time she told me my hamster died.

My own voice scratches at my throat when I ask, "Mom is Loki okay?"

She chuckles and runs a hand through my hair. I clutch her hand in both of mine. The bandages on both my wrists make me realize what a blessing it is, being next to her.

"He was a bit scared due to the storm. But he's with Luke now. They're at Stella's."

I sigh in relief. Mom moves forward and adjusts my pillows, raising my bed up. I sit up, propped by the pillows, relieved again when my head doesn't throb with the movement. She picks up a glass of water from my bedside table and keeps a hold of it even when I take it. I gulp the cool liquid down my parched throat.

"That's enough."

I settle back as she takes the glass away from me.

"Detective Williams is waiting outside to ask you a few questions. Do you feel up to it?"

I gasp as everything suddenly hits me full speed. I have to tell her everything!

"Sadie? Mom, please call her in."

Mom signs at me to calm down before walking out. I take a deep breath, ready to tell Sadie all about Cora. She must be stopped before she hurts someone else. Sadie comes in. Though her clothes are dry, her wet hair is gathered up in a bun.

"Sadie! It was Cora!" I blurt out as soon as I see her. "She was—"

It takes me by surprise when she doesn't stop until she has her arms around me in a tight hug. Before I can even hug her back, she backs a foot away. Her face is stoic, but I see her red-rimmed eyes.

"Sadie… are you okay?"

She smiles, "Are you seriously asking *me* that? I'm not the one in a hospital bed."

"I can't feel a thing," I grin and try to wink at her.

"I'm sorry I didn't act on your doubts about Cora."

"It's not your fault."

She nods, then takes out a notepad from her pocket.

"If you could recount everything for me, that would be great."

"I was abducted from my bakery. I don't know where she took me because I was unconscious. She planned to frame me for Marco's death. I riled her up a bit so she would mess up, but she hit me instead. I was immediately unconscious and when I came to, she wasn't there. We have to find her Sadie. She is angry and desperate. She will hurt anyone to get away."

She sighs, pinching her brow between her fingers.

"What is it?" I ask when she doesn't say anything.

"Did Cora tell you how she found the wolfsbane plant?"

"She said—" I frown, trying to remember what it was that she said. "I'm not sure."

"Do you remember who found you?"

My frown deepens. Flashes of darkness and loud, thunderous rain come and go. I close my eyes to hold onto a clearer memory.

"I was alone. I— I called for help. But… was it Detective Roberts?"

I am surprised when she nods, even more surprised by what she says next.

"Cora is in jail. She confessed. She was the one who told us where you were."

"What? So it's over?"

She shakes her head. "She is arrested because she confessed to kidnapping you. Not Marco's murder."

"But it was her! She has the plant. She attacked me when I said she'll go to jail for it."

"She attacked you because she panicked. She wasn't trying to frame you. She thought you were trying to frame her."

"That's what she wants you to believe."

She shakes her head, as if clearing her thoughts.

"Lily, Aiden knows."

"Knows what?"

"He knows we were working together."

I recall my encounter with him on my birthday.

"Is he okay with that?"

Her eyes widen, "*Okay?* Lily, I've never seen him angrier than he was when he found out you were missing. He told me that I put a civilian life at risk and he is absolutely right."

"He isn't. I did what I felt was right. And I would've done everything I could to find Marco's killer, with or without you. I'm just thankful that you decided to take a chance and help me."

She nods, but I know she's not convinced. I open my mouth to speak, but she beats me to it.

"You should rest now. Grampa asked me to give you his best wishes and that he'll visit you when you're better. He misses you."

"I miss him too. I just wanted to be done with this whole thing before I saw him again so no one would isolate him for being associated with me."

"You didn't have to worry about that. He doesn't care."

"But I do. Just like I care about finding the killer—"

"I'm sorry, I really have to go. Thank you for your time, Miss Grayson."

Worry twists my gut as she leaves. I have to make sure she doesn't get in any trouble with Detective Roberts. We still have a murder to solve. And then there's Cora. Is Sadie right about her? Why can't I remember what she said? What else do I not remember?

The door opens again and my Dad rushes in followed by Mom. Dad hugs me tightly like Sadie did. I hug him back, grateful to all that is holy for giving me the chance to do it again.

"I love you Dad."

He squeezes me tighter, "I love you more, Lil."

Chapter 17

Chapter 17

After a day of resting and being fussed over, I assure my parents that I'm fine. They test me multiple times for a concussion. I pass all of them with flying colors. When they finally drop me off at home, I take Loki inside and spend some time playing with him, giving him the much needed and deserved attention. His gallop eventually slows down to a prowl and he ends up on the foot of my bed. I kneel next to him and pet the soft fur of his head, watching him slow-blink at me.

"I'm sorry I left you all alone in the storm. You must have been so scared. I was too."

He licks my finger when I tap his nose.

"I'm going to fight for a friend. Wish me luck. But I'll be back soon. I'll even bring your favorite tuna jelly."

A meow rumbles out of his stomach at that, making me chuckle. I kiss his head and get to my feet.

"See ya!"

I bundle myself up in a thick sweater and grab the longest coat I own before locking my door and walking out. Somehow the cold I felt in the shed hasn't left me yet. I feel it tingling at my fingertips at the most random moments. Eyeing the dark clouds still looming in the starless night sky, I put the coat in the basket of my bicycle and put a raincoat on instead.

"Lily!"

I whirl around, clutching my pounding heart.

"Jesus, Polly!" I gasp for air.

Her usually pinned up hair bounces in big, loose curls around her face as she jogs up to me and gathers me in a hug.

"I was so worried about you when I heard what happened!" She cups my cheeks in her hands, after her fingers brush the bandage on the side of my forehead. "Why didn't you call me?"

I lower her hands away from my face as I answer her, "I was at my parents' house. They feared I had a concussion and shouldn't be left alone."

"Have you heard? Cora got arrested. You have nothing to be scared of anymore."

I smile, "I'm not afraid, Polly, but I won't rest until Marco's killer is behind bars."

Her face falls. "Cora didn't do it?"

"The police are not sure yet. Though I'm sure they'll reach a conclusion soon."

She quietly nods, her lips pulled into a thin smile. "Are you going somewhere?"

"Yeah, umm..." I try to think of a good excuse. "Groceries!"

"Don't bother. Have dinner at my place tonight."

My stomach twists at the thought of spending time with anyone except Loki for a few days. Though I try to tell myself that it's just Polly and I've had dinner with her countless times, I still don't feel right in my bones.

"My parents want me to spend the night at their place again. I just wanted to pick up a few things from home before I go back."

She raises an eyebrow, clearly not buying it, but gets out of my way.

"Sure, some other time then. Be safe now."

I wave goodbye at her as I pedal away. The ride to the precinct is thankfully uneventful. Once again, I give myself a pep talk in the parking lot while putting on my coat, before going inside. The old receptionist smiles when I wave at her. Knowing my way this time around, I don't stop for help. The station is abuzz even in the late evening.

No light filters out from beneath Detective Roberts's closed office door. One who hasn't been there before would think that he's not in, but I know better. I knock on his door.

"Enter."

I open the door to a slit and peek inside before opening the door fully. Sure enough, his desk is littered with files and papers and a spare suit hangs on the cabinet's knob. I am surprised to notice in the dim light that the man does eat, for an empty takeout container sits on his side table.

"You better have an excellent reason for being out of bed."

I nod absent-mindedly, before I realize what he said. I look at him— his deep frown to be exact.

"I do, actually."

He stands up, his gait stony, as if he'd been sitting there for a long time. Walking around his desk, he takes out the chair in front of it and gestures at the seat.

"Have a seat."

Agreeing, I go to sit but some deep-rooted instinct stops me at the idea of sitting in the *chair* with its back to the door; the only entrance to this room.

"Of course," the detective mutters, "I'm sorry."

He picks up the chair and places it against the wall, right next to the side table, now facing his desk *and* the door. Resisting the urge to hug him, I take the seat and he goes back behind his desk.

"Thank you."

"It's nothing. I should have been more aware. It is basic—"

"I meant for saving me." I cut him off before he reduces it to nothing.

His eyelashes dust the top of his cheeks as his eyes lower down.

"I didn't save you, Miss Grayson. I merely found you where your kidnapper said you'd be. Had you not created that noise, I wouldn't even have found you on time." I notice the lack of the usual spark in his eyes when he looks at me again. "So, if you want to thank someone, thank yourself."

"I will."

He nods, "Good."

"But that doesn't mean that I can't thank you."

His eyes narrow slightly. Mine follow suit. I resolve to not be the one to look away first. He must notice my determination because he averts his gaze the very next second, his face scrunching up in annoyance.

"Are you mad?" I ask, immediately wanting to lift him up.

"No."

"Your face is all scrunched up," I bring up my hands and claw them around my face, imitating his expression.

The lines on his forehead deepen. "It's not."

"It's okay if you're mad."

"I'm. Not. Mad."

"Great!" I perk up. "Can you tell Sadie that too?"

His scowl disappears as his lips part in surprise. "What?"

"Tell her that you're not mad at us for being in cahoots together."

I note the return of his scowl with great defeat.

"I'm not in the habit of lying."

"Detective Roberts, I'm sure I didn't get into trouble because of Sadie. I am a grown woman and I make my own choices. If Sadie didn't have my back, I would've done anything, how ever reckless, to prove Cora was behind it all."

With his fingers steepled together, he leans forward on the table.

"And how are you so sure that it was Cora?"

"I overheard her talking on the phone one morning."

"And did she confess her first-degree murder on a phone call?"

My face twists— when he puts it like that it does sound idiotic.

"No she did not. But she did say that she messed up with Marco and that she will not make the same mistake twice."

"That does sound *dubious*, Miss Grayson. But it does not confirm anything. In my line of work, I cannot act on impulse. I need proof before I can pin someone for a crime they may have committed."

His words strike a chord. How do I tell him that more often than not, my impulses turn out to be true? Like when I *just knew* Charlie was cheating on me. I turned out to be correct after a series of tests. But I try to convince him the only way I know he can be; with facts.

"She is a botanist. She knows all there is to know about plants. I think she is the only one clever enough to have burned Marco's tongue so he wouldn't feel the bitter taste. There was a book about poisonous plants in her shop. Though that's not substantial enough because it belongs to Mr. Williams's library. She has been trying to shift blame on me since the day Marco died. Because she is vindictive. She always has been. Also, in case you didn't notice, she did kidnap me and left me for dead."

He bristles, "And she is sitting in jail for that."

"Are you really going to believe that she didn't kill Marco?"

He sighs, rubbing his forehead. I sense his internal struggle. It isn't difficult to. With another long exhale, he leans close again, speaking in a low voice.

"She showed us footage of someone breaking into her shop and placing that plant there. We got a call too. But she must have hid it when one of our officers went to investigate."

I quickly get over my shock about him sharing information with me and ask him the first question that pops into my head.

"Who made the call?"

"It was from a burner phone."

I fall back. Another dead end.

"Why hide it if she wasn't guilty?"

"Vindictive, like you said," he shrugs.

"And where's the plant now?"

"Somewhere safe."

I rub my chin, deep in thought. He lets me think in peace and silence.

"I want to meet her." I announce, standing up.

He immediately shakes his head. "Absolutely not."

"I wasn't asking."

"Miss Grayson," he stands up too, "please, you don't need to see her again."

"I have to."

I hear his chair scratching the floor as he quickly follows me outside. I stop when I see the nearest officer and ask him to show me to the cells.

"I'll handle it, Jones."

Jones, the officer, nods at Detective Roberts behind me. Making it clear where his loyalty lies, he completely ignores me and instantly takes his leave. Knowing Detective Roberts would try to talk me out of it again, I don't wait around for him to 'handle it'. I take the first left towards the only corridor I haven't seen yet. Detective Roberts effortlessly keeps pace with my brisk walk.

"Why are you so adamant on seeing her?"

"She tried to kill me. She owes me an explanation at least."

I do indeed find the jail cells at the end of the hallway. It is a sight that stops me in my tracks.

"Miss Grayson—"

"This is certainly cleaner than I imagined. Are all the cells like this?" I point at the one in front of me.

I inch forward to see who is in there, but I'm stopped by a hand on my elbow.

"I'll bring Cora in to meet you." Detective Roberts gestures at a door on the far side of the hall. "Wait in that room over there."

I look at him pointedly, knowing he just steered me off course. However, I don't argue with him as he is finally doing what I want. I take the path he steers me towards and enter the white, clinical room. It is very similar to the interrogation room I found myself in twice.

I'm still pacing when Detective Roberts returns with Sadie and a handcuffed Cora in tow. She sneers as soon as she sees me. Her wild hair, her scowl, her likeness to my ex-husband, and her willingness to kill me, makes my blood boil.

"What the hell is *she* doing here?"

My feet move past the detective on their own accord and before I know it, my fist snaps out, hitting Cora right under her jaw. I feel it snap together beneath my knuckles and hear her teeth clack. I wait for the satisfaction of hitting her to come but before it does, both the detectives jump in. Sadie pulls Cora back while Aiden tugs at me.

I don't resist the pull. Uneasiness settles in my gut, and I try to make up with words what I couldn't with my fist, hoping they'll at least bring me the satisfaction I crave.

"What did you say again?" I address Cora as she tries to maneuver the handcuffs to clutch her aching jaw, "That I couldn't land a blow on you? That you'll end me a thousand times before I could? Well, in case it didn't hurt enough, *that* was a blow."

"Li—Miss Grayson," I hear Detective Roberts's soft voice from behind my back, "I understand what you've been through, but it would be great if you could refrain from assault."

I flip my hair over my back and take a seat at the table in the middle of the room. Sadie looks at her partner in question. He nods. She tries to steer Cora towards the table too, but when she doesn't budge, Sadie shoves her ahead.

"I don't want to be here with this bitch!" Cora whines.

She isn't given an answer as she is lowered into the chair in front of me. The detectives step to the side, but don't leave the room. She huffs and claps her handcuffs on the table.

"What do you want?"

"For you to admit that you killed Marco."

If looks could kill, I'd be six feet under too.

"I didn't," she seethes.

"Yeah," I scoff, "right. You've always been a bully. Who's to say that your skills didn't develop into something more heinous after school?"

Cora's eyes narrow to slits. "You think you're so holier-than-thou, don't you? With all your fancy clothes," she waves her handcuffed wrists in the air around me, as she speaks through gritted teeth, "and your people pleasing act. That no one can ever come close to deserve your company or attention. But if you ever deign to actually look around you, you'd notice that people are *real* people. They have lives too. Marco was my friend too. I cared for him as he did for me. I've known—" I watch, shocked, as tears gather in her eyes. "*I knew* him for thirteen years. Far longer than you did. I am not above admitting that I made a mistake in abducting and hitting you. But I still don't regret trying to find who killed him."

With the last word, she snaps her lips shut and moves back in her seat, realizing she said too much. Meanwhile, I sit in my astonishment. I don't think I have ever seen her so emotive before. Suddenly feeling a bit woozy, I stand up. My mouth opens to say something but my tongue locks up in uncertainty. Cora looks up then. Even with the tears lacing her eyes, there is anger in there. She glares, but I have no idea how I know that it is not *at* me. My head swims, the cold numbness at my fingertips, travelling up my arms. I decide I should leave before our silence enters the psychopath territory.

Right as I leave, the floor and walls all turn to jelly around me. I touch the nearest one to stabilize myself.

"Miss Grayson?"

I turn around to face Detective Roberts. *His pale eyes aren't jelly*, I am relieved to note.

"Jail is no fun, I tell you."

He looks at me, surprised, "You've been to jail?"

I nod, "In Monopoly."

A small smile quirks up his lips but disappears again after a glance at my face.

"Are you okay?"

"Yeah."

"You sure? Because you look like you're about to pass out."

The second he mentions it, I realize what is wrong with me.

"Yeah," I gasp out the words, "maybe I am."

My knees crumble beneath me. His voice calling out my name echoes somewhere against the jelly walls.

Chapter 18

Chapter 18

My eyes thank whoever was considerate enough to dim the lights of the room I'm in, before roaming the familiar space. Sadie's office is as neat as ever, not a thing out of its place. Except the tall, iron rod next to the couch I'm lying on. I lift my hand, noticing the IV line inserted and taped to the back, my knuckles slightly bruised.

"Don't move it around too much."

I tilt my head up to look at Sadie upside down. Her chair rolls across the floor as she moves from the head of the couch to the side.

"My knuckles are swollen."

She smirks, "You should see Cora's face, Laila Ali."

I groan, rubbing my own face. My mind juggles memories; both recent and old. Flashbacks of Aiden's worried eyes in the dingy shed, Cora's hard gaze and panicked pacing, and finally Sadie sheltering us with an umbrella until the ambulance arrived revolve in my head.

"You're lucky she isn't pressing charges."

I sit up, waves of nausea radiating through my head. Sadie grabs my shoulders as I sway on the spot.

"Whoa, Lily, are you sure you're not concussed?"

I nod and point at my pricked hand, "Dehydrated maybe. But definitely not concussed."

"Just stay put," she slowly leans me back against the couch.

I get back to the point as soon as the queasiness subsides.

"When is her hearing?"

"Tomorrow, I think. Why do you ask?"

"How long is she going to jail for?"

"Two years minimum."

"If I drop all charges against her, will it affect her sentence?"

Sadie's eyebrows pull together at once.

"You really want to do that?"

A sigh escapes my lips as I remind myself of the truth I saw in Cora's eyes. She wasn't lying about being Marco's friend.

"Are you sure she didn't kill Marco?"

Sadie nods.

"Then yes, I really want to."

"As your friend, I don't think you should make this decision on a whim, Lily. Are you sure you're not just doing it because you feel guilty for punching her?"

"I don't feel guilty for punching her," I immediately deny.

She purses her lips and gives me a look. I sigh, *why does she know me that well?*

"I'll think it through just to appease you, but I don't think my decision will be any different."

"I don't get it," she frowns. "Why the sudden change of heart?"

"I get where she's coming from," I shrug. "I'm not saying that I would've done the same thing. But I get her motive. And if she hates me that much, it's really no shocker that she jumped at the chance to scare me a little."

"She didn't just scare you, Lily."

At a loss for words, I shut my eyes and rest my head back against the wall.

"And she was wrong, you know?"

"About what?"

"About you."

She continues when I look at her again.

"You do have really good taste in clothes," she smiles, making me smile too, "but you're not haughty. She was right on the nose with the people pleasing thing though. However, it's not your responsibility to know everything about everyone. Even I thought she was bullshitting everyone at the memorial to be honest."

"I know you're only trying to make me feel better."

"Is it working?"

I give her a tired smile and lean against the cushions. Cora didn't kill Marco. Which brings me back to square one. Was I right in questioning Max? With my heart throbbing painfully because I'm about to betray my friend, I sit up.

"Sadie there's some—"

The door to her office swings open after a sharp knock. A slim man with greyish hair walks in.

"Ah!" He grins at me. "The sleeping beauty awakens."

I look from him to Sadie.

"Lily, this is Dr. Steel, our precinct's private physician."

"That's a lot of P's Detective Williams," Dr. Steel chuckles as he checks the bottle hanging from the rod.

"Right on time. You're done here Miss Grayson."

He kneels down to take the needle out of my hand. I look at Sadie as he does. I might not be scared of needles but it's no pleasure to see one enter or exit my body. The crinkle of a plastic wrapper brings my gaze back to him.

"Here you go."

I look at the lollipop in his hand then back at him.

"I'm thirty," I state.

"You can have water too, but this," he raises the lolly in his hand, "is a must, I'm afraid."

Sadie snickers in her seat. I roll my eyes at her and take the lolly from him.

"Thank you."

"You're very welcome, my dear."

With that, he stands up and picks up a briefcase from the floor.

"I'll walk you out," Sadie moves to stand up.

"Oh no," Dr. Steel motions her to sit, "Aiden will do it. He's the one who dragged me here. He might as well be the one to send me on my way."

Sadie grins like a cat who got the canary.

"He really did, didn't he? He's not usually like that. Don't know what got into him."

Dr. Steel answers her with a smile and a pointed look over his glasses.

"See you later, Sadie." He turns and bows at me, "Miss Grayson."

I wave at him with my left, non-achy hand.

"Thanks again, Dr. Steel."

After he leaves, I smack Sadie's arm.

"Ow!" She yelps, rubbing at her arm. "You're awfully vicious today, aren't you?"

"Only for people who deserve it! Why were you making fun of Detective Roberts? He's a good man."

"Whenever did I say he's not? In fact, he's always so calm. The first time I saw him lose his composure was the night you got kidnapped. Your partner, Max, called us almost an hour before Cora showed up."

"Max?" I sit up, "What did he say? Did you talk to him? How did he sound?"

"Calm down Sherlock! He said that you both were at the bakery and he went out to make a call. When he came back, you weren't there and he found your phone smashed in the alley. I didn't talk to him so I don't know how he sounded then, but I met with him afterwards and he was pretty shaken up. He even came by the hospital when you were still unconscious. Haven't you seen him since?"

"He visited my parents' yesterday, with Stella of all people. But I was asleep so they left."

She nods at my face, "You're frowning pretty hard over there."

"Sadie," I sigh, "I was so sure Cora was the one who poisoned Marco. If she didn't do it, then who did?"

She places her hand on mine. "We'll find out soon, Lily. Whoever it is, they can't run forever. But I need you to stay out of it. Please."

A nod is all I can manage for her at the moment.

"I'd like to go home now."

"I'll drop you off."

We run into Detective Roberts in the parking lot. His dark hair shines, slightly wet from the drizzle. It's a welcome reprieve; the rain, not his hair. Though the latter is not an unwanted sight either.

"Miss Grayson." He halts in his tracks when he sees us. "How are you feeling now?"

"Much better. Thank you."

Sadie's loud ringtone jars me.

"Sorry Lily, I have to get this. Hey Aiden, can you drop her home please?"

She runs back inside without waiting around for any of us to reply. As she disappears, I turn back to the detective.

"Detective Roberts, you don't have to—"

I jump at the beep of a car unlocking. When I see the blinking lights but no one around us anywhere, I turn to him again. Only to see him shaking his head.

"What?"

"That's my car. Get inside before you get wet."

Ignoring the weird urge to laugh, I point at my bicycle.

"That's my bike. I can go—"

"It'll be at your house first thing in the morning. Anything else?"

I glare at his annoyingly handsome frown and stomp to his car. My glare only intensifies when he's there before I am, to open the door for me. I get in, immediately wrapped in the rich scent of sandalwood and leather. Crossing my arms, I watch as he rounds the car and gets in the driver's seat.

"Put on your seatbelt."

My glare doesn't lessen at the order. He notices my noncompliance after turning the heater up a notch.

"Miss Grayson, I won't ask again."

"I didn't hear you asking in the first place."

His eyebrows jump up his forehead.

"You want me to say please for trying to make sure you're safe in case of an accident? Is that what this is?"

I feel my cheeks burn up in embarrassment, but I hold my ground.

"Maybe," I shrug.

He huffs, a small smile peeking out, or maybe just my delusion. My heart gallops in my chest as he leans forward across the console and looks into my eyes.

"I know it's hard for you, but try to be self-preservative sometimes for your own sake, *please*."

The click of my seatbelt being locked into place breaks me out of the stupor. I blink away from his capturing gaze and lean back, realizing I had unconsciously moved towards him.

"Heterochromatic."

"Sorry?"

I curse at myself for speaking out loud.

"You have heterochromatic eyes," I stupidly state the fact he obviously already knows.

He nods as his cheeks tinge with pink and backs the car out of the precinct. Meanwhile, I look outside the window and try not to think about his striking eyes.

Stopped at a red light, I suddenly remember what he said earlier.

"Wait a damn minute!"

He turns to me wide-eyed, hands gripping the wheel.

"What do you mean, *it's hard for me*?!"

He breathes at that, his shoulders relaxing.

"When have I given you the impression of being reckless? I'll have you know that I am very cautious and a level-headed person."

"Are you serious right now?" He shakes his head while looking at me.

"Do I look like I'm joking?"

The light turns green at that very moment. He drives ahead, muttering something under his breath. We pass the gates to the neighbourhood I live in.

I gesture out of the window, "It's a left from here."

He takes a right. I glare at his profile.

"Did you do that on purpose?"

His jaw twitches as he clenches his teeth. I don't get why he is so angry. Come to think of it, I don't even know why *I'm* so angry.

"Take another right—"

He speeds up and goes straight ahead.

"We're going towards a dead end."

Instead of answering, he takes the dirt road into the forest. My heart jumps into my throat.

"Oh my god. You're going to kill me here, aren't you?"

I'm surprised when a glance at his face shows me his breath-taking grin.

"Are you laughing at me?"

He keeps smiling like that and I soon forget that I'm supposed to be scared. The dirt road clears out and he takes another right to stop right at the back of my house.

Will he ever stop being surprising?

He turns off the ignition and faces me.

"You're neither cautious nor level-headed."

I open my mouth to protest but he shushes me with a finger to my lips. Stunned into silence, I watch as he quickly lowers his hand and covers it with the other.

"What you are is vexing and a pain in the ass because you decided to insert yourself in an ongoing police investigation with no regards to how that could endanger you. And it *has* endangered you. Had it been the real killer, you could've been nex—" closing his eyes, he pinches the bridge of his nose.

I don't dare speak, astounded by how affected he is. After a steadying breath, he continues.

"You need to understand that finding Marco's killer is not your responsibility. It is mine. I don't want you or anyone else interfering in my job. Having civilians doing stupid things and putting themselves at risk only diverts my attention from the main aim. Do you understand?"

I'm about to nod, because I can relate with wanting to do my job on my own, until he opens his mouth again.

"Just stick with baking and being pretty, and stay out of police investigations."

I rear back. "You did *not* just say that."

He starts the car again, clearly avoiding my eyes.

"I did." He adds as an afterthought, "And I mean it."

A beat passes while I wait for him to take it back, something vile crawling at the back of my throat. When he doesn't, I unclip my seatbelt.

"Very well, Detective Roberts. This vexing civilian won't be getting in your way anymore. Maybe I wouldn't even have to if you were any good at your job."

He flinches but doesn't look my way again as I get out of the damned car that smells like him way too much.

Chapter 19

Chapter 19

I spend the night curled up next to Loki and the next day in my PJs. Refusing to wallow another day, I put on my joggers and go for a run.

It's a battle convincing myself that I don't care what the annoying detective thinks of me. He has another thing coming if he thinks that 'baking and being pretty' is all I'm good for. The reptilian part of my brain slithers again at the reminder of him calling me pretty but I slam it down.

Back from the run, I see Polly lugging out a huge garbage bag. She stops in surprise as she sees me on the driveway.

"Lily! I didn't expect you to be running again so soon. How are you doing?"

I stop near the flower pots lining our boundary.

"I'm good. Do you need any help with that?"

She laughs, flipping her luscious, wavy hair over her shoulder.

"Oh no, no I've got it. It's just one of those days, you know?" she winks.

I smile, not having a single clue what she means. She hops forward and I head towards my door.

"Hey Lily?"

"Yeah?"

"Whatever became of Cora? Is she going away for Marco's murder?"

I look over my shoulder. She stands there clutching the bag and biting her lip, attention fully on me again.

"She was proven innocent, but since she did kidnap me, she got sentenced to eight months in prison."

She nods, her gaze unfocused as she thinks about something.

"See you tomorrow," I move to go in, hearing Loki meowing from inside.

"Oh you might not, I'm leaving to stay with my parents in New York."

"Really?" I turn back to her. "For how long?"

"A while," she shrugs. "Mom broke her leg."

"Oh. Well if—"

"Hey, why don't we have dinner together tonight? I'll bring over pasta and wine. You can make dessert. What say you?"

"I'm in."

She smiles, "See ya!"

***

I'm mixing icing when the house phone rings. Mindful of the moisturizing mask on my face, I pick up the receiver.

"Hello?"

"Bamboo!" Stella squeals. "You're not going to believe what just happened!"

Wincing, I put the phone on speaker and lower the volume.

"Try me," I say as I pick up the bowl again.

"I went by the hospital this morning to drop off Ryan's breakfast. It was pandemonium!"

"What happened, Stel?"

I suddenly regret not leaving the house for two days after hearing the excitement in her rushed words.

"Now don't ask how I know all of this. It's all from credible sources and you can hash it out with Sadie later."

"About that—"

"Your detective was after Frank for the longest time for embezzlement and tax evasion. Someone from the precinct revealed that he's about to put out an arrest warrant soon. So Frank had him attacked by his goonies late last night. He's at the hospital..."

The whisk drops from my hand. Her voice fades beneath the blood roaring in my ears. I pick up the phone.

"...Ryan said it—"

"Aiden was attacked?" My voice trembles.

"Yeah. But luckily, he got it all on footage and used it to have Frank arrested. But get this, just before his arrest, Frank cornered Polly at the grocery store. He made a whole scene. Called her a liar and cheater. Said that he won't be keeping her secrets anymore. He only backed off when she warned him that she knows just as much. He barely made it out of the store when the police arrived."

Every bit of information fragments into memories of past events and clues I didn't imagine to explore sooner. I cannot believe I was only looking at facts and not going deeper than them. To tell the truth, I was trying so hard to think and act like a detective.

But I'm not.

I am an outsider who did everything to fit in. That includes paying attention to things no one else was.

"You still there?"

I look at the clock. It's almost six-thirty. "When did all this happen?"

"Around two p.m. I think."

"Stella, I have dinner with Polly at eight."

"Oh am I keeping you?"

With the plan forming in my head, I utter the words I seldom ever do.

"I need your help."

***

Drying myself off from the quick but necessary shower, I put band-aids on the scratches at my legs from my impromptu trek. I had taken out the little black dress that works for me every single time. But looking at my legs, I second guess it. The sound of the doorbell propels me into motion. In record time, I pull the dress up, take the rollers out of my hair, and put on lipstick before rushing outside.

Hiding my breathlessness with my best sultry smile, I open the door. Polly stands there with a dish in one hand and a wine bottle in the other.

"Oh dear, have you started the party without me?" she grins. "You look absolutely flushed."

I chuckle, trying to mask my nervousness, and let her in. As she makes her way to the kitchen, I crack open the window in the living room. She sets both things on the table. Loki jumps up, curiously sniffing at the new objects. I watch his eyes squinting as he smells the bottle more closely. A split second later he rears back and hisses. Polly tuts and waves him off the table.

Pretending to not have seen anything, I sway into the kitchen and sidle up next to her. Her head tilts as she looks at me. I smile before turning around.

"Can you tie me up?"

I hear her choke on air.

"Do you need water?"

"No, I'm good," she coughs and starts tying the knot supposed to hold my dress together at the back.

When her fingers stroke my revealed skin, I step away, picking up two glasses and a bottle from my own fridge.

"I hope you don't mind but I plan on getting drunk today, and that bottle alone isn't going to cut it."

"Amen to that," she grins and picks up her bottle too.

"Why don't you put that in the fridge?"

She stops and looks my way. I get an inkling that she feels something is up. Her eyes narrow and I know whatever comes next is a test.

"It's chilled enough if we have it first."

I put the bottle in my hand back into the fridge.

"Sure."

She eases back and I walk out into the living room. Once we're settled, she pours out our drinks. My heart clenches as I lose my mind at not having control over the situation. She hands me my glass and sits back with hers.

"So when are you driving out?"

"I leave at Dawn," she replies, glancing at the unsipped drink in my hands.

I nod and lift the glass up, thinking of ways to pretend to take a sip. Suddenly the bell rings. In my hurry to escape, I stand up too fast and end up spilling my drink all over Polly's lavender dress. She screeches and shoots to her feet.

"I'm so sorry!" I gasp.

Her fists tight at her sides, and her face burning with anger, she puts down her glass.

"You can wash up in the restroom, Polly. I'm so sorry. I'll give you something to change into."

She inhales and lets go. "It's okay, give me a minute."

I go to the front door as she walks inside. Hannah appears as nervous as I feel. The milkmaid braids on her head and the buttoned-up floral sundress are so starkly different from Polly's bouncy curls and revealing silk dress. For the first time, the contrast between her and Polly is visible to me.

"Are you ready?" I ask her.

She nods and hurries inside, shutting the door behind her.

"We don't have to say anything," I whisper. "She's in the restroom."

Loki meows at my feet. I pick him up and quickly shut him inside my bedroom, not wanting him to get caught in the crosshairs. The second I step back into the hallway, I hear the restroom door open. Determination crosses Hannah's eyes and we share a second of calm, before leaping at each other as planned. Her lips are surprisingly soft, but her hands are not. They squeeze my butt as I cage her against the door. I swallow the bile down my throat and don't have to fake the teary-eyed look when I'm forcefully pushed away from her. I step closer to the wall of the living room.

"What the hell?!" Polly roars, her chest heaving as if she was the one making out.

"I can explain—" I begin but don't get very far.

Polly's fingers clasp my throat and I'm shoved against the wall.

"Polly leave her alone!"

Polly keeps a hold of my throat, turning to Hannah. "Explain. NOW!"

"We don't owe you anything!" Hannah bursts out in anger.

"*We?*"

"She's always treated me as an equal and given me respect. Something you never did," Hannah sobs.

Polly sneers at her, "I've burned my whole world for you!"

"For YOU!" Hannah tries to push her off me. "Everything you ever do is for you!"

Polly tightens her grip on my throat and hands.

"You're something else, aren't you? Going around, seducing my girlfriend. And here I thought you're a clueless little thing."

"Is that... why... you're framing me?" I gasp as she cuts off my air completely.

Hannah pulls Polly's hair, causing her grip to falter. I force my hands out and push her hands off me. We all end up on the floor. Wheezing, I rub my throat to get some air down to my lungs.

"You bitch!" Polly backhands Hannah. "I loved you! I left my husband for you! And *this* is how you pay me back?"

I grab her hand before she can hit Hannah again.

"You left Frank because he abused you," I rasp, dragging her into the living room.

She bites my hand to free herself, punching the back of my knee. As I fall to the ground, she climbs on top of me. My cheek stings sharply under her palm.

"I learned a thing or two from him, so watch your mouth."

Hannah steps ahead. Polly's focus shifts from me to her.

"Did you also learn how to grow Wolfsbane from him?"

"Oh no honey," she leers, "that was all me."

Hannah's mouth wobbles as she forms her next words.

"Did you get the seeds when we went on our trip last year?"

"Really fell in love with me then, didn't you? That's when I decided I *have* to have you."

"Even if it meant killing Marco?" I manage to whisper.

Her thumb presses down at the base of my throat. Dark spots dance in front of my eyes.

"Even if it means killing you."

"You'll have to get out of jail first."

Polly startles at the fourth voice in the room, while I breathe in relief as her hands release me. Sadie socks her right in the jaw and too quickly for her to even comprehend it, she handcuffs Polly's hands behind her back.

Stella jumps in from outside the window where she was recording everything, and kneels to the ground beside me.

"Are you okay? Can you breathe?"

I nod. Hannah slumps onto the couch. Sadie gives me a thumbs up. I fall on my back.

It's finally over.

Thank you for reading Crumbling Deception! If you loved this book, I know you'll love the first book in my Misadventures of a Cat Detective series, **Claws and Conundrums**!

Read it here!

Little did I know that a mischievous tabby cat would become my ticket to freedom, using his uncanny ability to grant me visions and help me solve a perplexing murder where I'm the prime suspect!

Read it here!

Sneak Peek –

Chapter 1: The Letter to No One

I've died and gone to heaven.

My mind is reeling from the notion that I just became the owner of a historic mansion overnight. This cannot be real.

I'm very certain that I'm not related to the owner of a mansion in a town I've never visited.

I mean, I don't think I've ever even met the guy! *This must be a joke!*

But two days after receiving a thick, official-looking envelope, I find myself driving to the small town where my sudden good fortune came from.

Picklesquare? Who names a town Picklesquare? Why don't people answer phones here?

"Ugh." I can smell the cabbie's breath from here. He's nice enough, but a shower would do him a world of good.

He suddenly slams on the brakes.

"What? Is something wrong?" I ask in alarm.

"Nothing ma'am. Just don't want to run over anyone."

"Huh?" It takes a second to register, but when I look out the car window, all I see are flashes of bright colors.

The town is buzzing with excitement, full of vibrant colors, loud noises, and yummy smells.

Impatiently, I silently wish the cab had a siren. I could check out the festival after getting to Mr. Livingstone's mansion. The town is as interesting as it is peculiar, but I need to get to him to get the answer to my seemingly random inheritance.

"Wha—?" Something catches my eye, and I turn my gaze to it.

A bunch of teenagers nearby are throwing rotten oranges at a black Ford in the opposite lane. They look mischievous and are laughing like it is the funniest thing ever to pelt a car with a rotten orange.

Boys. Who's driving that car? How enraged are they that they will now need to clean rotten fruit off their car?

I turn to look at the cabbie, David. He doesn't even seem phased. He just chuckles and looks at me through the rearview mirror. He leans back. "People only throw rotten things at you if they hate you, you know."

I don't even like cleaning the dust or dew off my car.

I squint at the vehicle. "Who's in the car? The devil? Hitler incarnate?"

"I have no idea." The crowd finally thins out and he lurches the cab forward, jolting me back against my seat.

As the cab eases its way through the fading chaos of what I think is a Rotten Fruit Festival, my mind shifts to the task awaiting me at Mr. Livingstone's mansion. Two days ago, that unexpected letter arrived at my doorstep without an addressee.

Inside, I found a stack of documents bearing my name—titles to a grand estate just a few hours from my apartment. The top letter was odd and rubbed me the wrong way.

I hope this meets you in peace.

I am writing to you with a proposition of utmost significance. Enclosed within this envelope, you will find legal documents pertaining to the magnificent mansion of Mr. Livingstone. It may come as a surprise, but destiny has chosen you as the rightful heir to this grand estate.

You see, Mr. Livingstone has no immediate family. In his final moments of mental clarity, he entrusted me with the responsibility of locating the deserving owner of his beloved mansion. Through an extensive search and meticulous considerations, fate has guided me to you.

The moment I laid eyes on your name, I knew you were the one meant to inherit this glorious property. Your reputation as a person of integrity, wisdom, and compassion has reached far and wide, aligning perfectly with the values cherished by Mr. Livingstone throughout his life.

By signing the enclosed documents now, you will not only assume ownership of the mansion but also become the steward of its history and the legacy it holds.

Yours Faithfully,

Anna Butler

The Estate's Lawyer

As the cab jolts along the bumpy road, my mind wanders from "where in the heck my reputation was the topic of conversation" to the serene view out of the cab window. I watch the scenery change from the chaos of the fruit festival to a serene and quiet atmosphere. David slows to a stop opposite the town center, and I peer out the window, my eyes widening at the sight before me.

A lofty double gate with an inscription mounted at the top and written in bold letters "LIVINGSTONE ESTATE" stares back at me. The grounds alone are magnificent. A spiraling wonder of bushes across the open gate makes me realize how poor I am living in the confines of my shabby two-bedroom flat in New York City. A straight cobblestone road lined with trees, their branches reaching out to form a natural canopy overhead, leads to the front view of the estate. Here, green ferns and plants line the area, adding to the jaw-dropping sight of the mansion further back on the estate.

This place is amazing, I think to myself as I gaze at the perfectly planted array. My eye catches a young man with heavily sun-kissed skin, tending to the garden on one side. He is tall with a muscled body that makes him look like a heavyweight champion. He waves at our cab and flashes me a friendly smile. *Does he wave at every single person who passes by the garden?*

The trees that line the road filter the sunlight, casting shadows on the ground as we move. There are also occasional benches and picnic tables inviting travelers to stop and take a break along the outside of the gate.

"Here we are." David makes an abrupt stop in front of the mansion.

I reach into my purse and pull out some money to pay. David chuckles again. "You don't have to worry about that. I'm glad you're in Picklesquare and I hope you enjoy your time here."

"Well, that's very nice of you." Grateful, I slide my last few dollars back into my wallet.

"But be very careful in this part of town. Mr. Livingstone's mansion is the last place anyone visits in Picklesquare." His face darkens and his eyes no longer glisten.

I frown at his statement. "What do you mean by that?"

But before he can answer, a car drives into the compound and stops directly beside the cab. A black Ford with bits of fruit on its windshield. *The car at the festival!*

Out steps a young woman with fiery red hair. Her face is scrunched up in a deep frown as though she has been forced to gulp something bitter. She mumbles some words to herself and backs away from the car as if it were a piece of trash.

"Excuse me," I call out to her, hoping to find out how to avoid such a fiasco myself. "Are you alright?"

The woman turns to face me, her eyes narrowing in annoyance. "I'm fine. Just another day in Picklesquare where kids love to throw rotten fruit at my car. Well, I guess I'm glad it didn't end up like the last time..."

The last time was worse than this?

The red-haired woman must have seen the look on my face, urging her to tell me what had happened the last time. Her face breaks into a tired smile. "I don't think you need to know about that now. I'm Anna Butler, by the way. You seem to be from out of town. What's your name?"

Anna!

Here is the estate's lawyer, the same person who sent the letter to me. *Surely, she knows what's going on!*

"Charlotte Miller," I reply, returning the smile and trying to hide my anxiety.

Her eyes grow to the size of saucers, recognizing my name. "Charlotte, huh? You're the one who inherited Mr. Livingstone's mansion, right?"

I feel the scrutiny of her gaze as she takes in my petite frame, from the dark brown curls that fall across my face to the tennies shoes that adorn my feet. "Yes, but I believe there's been a mistake. I'm not related to Mr. Livingstone or..."

Anna interrupts me. "Let's go in, shall we?"

Unable to interject, I follow her up the stairs as David sets my luggage just inside the door. He vanishes without saying goodbye.

As soon as I enter the huge doors to the mansion, I feel like I've time-traveled to a fancy 18th-century plantation! The entrance hall has a cool wooden staircase and fancy designs on the ceiling that look like they are from a fairy tale. Sunlight peeks in through pretty stained-glass windows, making the rugs on the floor bask in a rainbow explosion.

The drawing room is all vintage vibes, with cozy velvet couches, fancy tables, and chandeliers that scream "upscale party." And the dining room? Oh boy! It has a massive wooden table that has probably seen more food than a buffet line.

And Mr. Livingstone wants to give me all this?

It couldn't be worse than a nightmare. I wouldn't know how to preserve the rugs from the dust of my shoes nor would I know how to save the velvet couches from being stained with my breakfast or lunch.

"This has to be a mistake," I whisper, taking in the magnificence of the room again and again.

Anna raises an eyebrow, placing her jacket carefully on the back of the couch. An amused smile plays on her lips now. "You think it's a mistake? I've been waiting for you. Did you bring the signed documents?"

I frown, trying to make sense of her words. "But why would I inherit anything from someone I'm not related to? I don't even know what he looks like!"

"Ah, that's the million-dollar question though, isn't it? You signed the documents though, right? It's important that you signed them," Anna says with a forced smile.

"No, I haven't. I want meet Mr. Livingstone because I do not intend to sign them. I still believe it is a mistake." I try not to shake.

Anna sighs, and I can see a frown returning to her face. *She is probably wishing the teenagers were still throwing rotten fruit at her. It would be better than facing an obstinate stranger who was rejecting a mansion!*

"Unfortunately, it's late now, and he doesn't receive visitors after sundown. You'll have to wait until morning. But I'll set you up in a room for the night."

"Very well. I suppose I understand. But I want to see Mr. Livingstone first thing tomorrow morning."

"That will not be a problem," Anna answers.

A sound soon echoes into the room where we are standing. I hear from the upper floor a "*tap tap*" that keeps on moving above us. I raise my head, "What's that?"

"Nothing," Anna quickly whispers, but I can tell from her voice that she is scared.

David's words ring in my head again. "*Mr. Livingstone's mansion is the last place anyone visits in Picklesquare.*"

The sound soon stops, again immersing us in the deep silence of the mansion's living room. I look at Anna but this time, her friendly smile is back on her face.

"Let me show you to your room." Anna walks out of the room.

We walk through a long passage that leads into the innermost part of the mansion. On each side of us, white stone walls adorned with intricate carvings line the passageway. The huge windows in the mansion go from the floor all the way up to the ceiling.

They must let in a lot of light during the day, offering a beautiful view of the outside scenery. It must make the rooms feel connected to nature.

"Here you go," Anna says as we get to a door in one of the hallways.

She opens it for me and steps aside, while gesturing to me to go inside. Greeted by the warmth of a big room that could comfortably take in my entire one-bedroom flat, my eyes feel permanently stuck open now. The furniture is antique but well-maintained and retains its original beauty.

The walls are adorned with beautiful paintings and intricate tapestries, and the floors are made of polished wood that gleam in the light from the lamp. The room is glorious, a reminder of a bygone era, a time when elegance and refinement were prized above all else. The big bed in the room is large enough for five people to fit across it, but still the room looks spacious.

As welcoming as the room feels, something seems a bit off. I shake off that feeling and continue touring the room with my eyes until Anna calls my name.

"Oh! Thanks," I reply as she opens the bathroom door on the left wall.

"The chef is running a warm bath for you. Also, tell her what you would like to eat for dinner."

I walk to the bed, running my hand over the comfy bedsheets. "Thank you." I sit down on the bed, barely knowing what to do with myself.

After a few minutes, a young lady in a white uniform and hair packed in a bun, knocks quietly on the bathroom door.

"Your bath is ready, Miss Miller," she announces, a polite smile stretching across her face.

Just like the gardener, she has no problem beaming at me as though we've been friends since forever. *Maybe this place isn't bad after all.*

"It's Charlotte. Are you the chef?"

"Yes'm, Diana Milligan, the chef of the Livingstone estate."

Diana leads me into the bathroom where a tub filled with water is waiting for me. The water is steaming and the bubbles smell like roses. Diana leaves and I hurriedly get into the water. I take a breath and try to relax, letting the water wash away my stress from the journey. It is so quiet in the bathroom that I can even hear myself breathing.

The bubbles feel really nice against my skin, like a soft massage tending to the knots in my muscles. I sink into the water and sigh.

Slipping into a ratty band shirt and shorts from high school, I feel completely underdressed standing in front of the mirror at the sink. I don't think these could be real gold faucets, but the vanity could certainly be real marble.

I don't want to leave, but I guess I'd have to buy a new wardrobe if I wanted to stay...

I must have spent almost an eternity in the tub because Diana has set out my evening meal on the table already by the time I get back into the room.

How did she already make this? I really thought she was bluffing when she said she could make my favorite meal.

I lift the plate cover to reveal a tender, juicy steak with a thick mushroom sauce. Roasted garlic mashed potatoes and a blend of seasonal vegetables are on another plate, with a chocolate lava cake on another.

It is the meal of royals, and today, I'm definitely living like one!

One bite and my taste buds are immediately awakened by the explosion of flavors. The food is expertly seasoned, with just the right amount of spices and herbs. I can tell that the ingredients are fresh and high-quality and that the dish has been prepared with care and attention to detail.

Perfection! I could get used to this...

As I dig into the food, I question why the mansion still seems off, despite its friendly inhabitants. I can't wait to meet Mr. Livingstone and hand over the documents and be free from this whole mansion debacle.

Even if I were the rightful heir, how am I supposed to keep this place up?

As I eat, I think about every possible reason that made Mr. Livingstone choose me to inherit his mansion. Nothing comes to my head as I had nothing that tied me to Picklesquare. Only my grandmother, who lived in this same town before her mysterious disappearance seventy years ago, could be a link. But my mom was taken to live with my aunt in Upstate New York shortly afterward, and we never came to visit this town after she had me.

Should I find Anna to say good night? She probably still hates me...

Thinking back to her car, I figure she might still be busy.

I'll just wait till morning to see her and Mr. Livingstone.

As I lay on my bed, my mind drifts to the life I have in New York City. I run a small bookstore, my sanctuary in the heart of a busy city. It is my haven filled with the amazing scent of old books and the soft rustle of pages turning. The cozy store is always adorned with stacks of novels, memoirs, and poetry collections, whispering tales of distant lands and captivating characters.

But it wasn't just the books that made the bookstore special. My cat, Clara, always lit up the place with her vibrant presence. Clara and I were like two peas in a pod, her furry paws always tagging along behind me.

This was until she died five months ago. Her death was a huge blow to me, and I haven't recovered from it. *I miss stroking Clara's fur and hearing her purr at the sight of me.*

But maybe things happen for a reason. Maybe fate has brought me to Mr. Livingstone's mansion for something I've yet to uncover.

Read it here!

My Favorite Banana Bread

Ingredients

- 2 cups (250g) **all-purpose flour** (spooned & leveled)

- 1 teaspoon **baking soda**

- 1/4 teaspoon **salt**

- 1/2 teaspoon **ground cinnamon**

- 1/2 cup (8 Tbsp; 113g) **unsalted butter**, softened to room temperature

- 3/4 cup (150g) packed light or dark **brown sugar**

- 2 large **eggs**, at room temperature

- 1/3 cup (80g) **plain yogurt** or **sour cream**, at room temperature

- 2 cups (460g) **mashed bananas** (about 4 large ripe bananas)

- 1 teaspoon **pure vanilla extract**

- optional: 3/4 cup (100g) chopped **pecans** or **walnuts**

Instructions

- Adjust the oven rack to the lower third position and preheat the oven to 350°F (177°C). Lowering the oven rack prevents the top of your bread from browning too much, too soon. Grease a metal 9×5-inch loaf pan with nonstick spray. Set aside.

- Whisk the flour, baking soda, salt, and cinnamon together in a medium bowl. Set aside.

- Using a handheld or stand mixer fitted with a paddle or whisk attachment, beat the butter and brown sugar together on high speed until smooth and creamy, about 2 minutes. With the mixer running on medium speed, add the eggs one at a time, beating well after each addition. Then beat in the yogurt, mashed bananas, and vanilla extract until combined.

- With the mixer running on low speed, slowly beat the dry ingredients into the wet ingredients until no flour pockets remain. Do not over-mix. Fold in the nuts, if using.

- Pour and spread the batter into the prepared baking pan. Bake for 60–65 minutes, making sure to loosely cover the bread with aluminum foil halfway through to prevent the top from getting too brown. The bread is done when a toothpick inserted in the center comes out clean with only a few small moist crumbs. This may be after 60–65 minutes depending on your oven, so begin checking every 5 minutes around the 60-minute mark.

- Remove bread from the oven and allow the bread to cool in the pan set on a wire rack for 1 hour. Remove bread from the pan and cool bread directly on the wire rack until ready to slice and serve.

- Cover and store banana bread at room temperature for 2 days or in the refrigerator for up to 1 week. Banana bread tastes best on day 2 after the flavors have settled together.

Notes

- **Butter:** If needed, you can use salted butter in this recipe with no other changes needed. I've also successfully reduced the butter down to 6 Tablespoons (85g) with no issue (just as tasty).

- **Brown Sugar:** This is not an overly sweet quick bread. If you want a sweeter banana bread, increase to 1 cup (200g) brown sugar. Feel free to replace some or all of the brown sugar with regular white granulated sugar.

- **Cream Cheese Frosting:** This banana bread also tastes fantastic with cream cheese frosting on top! To make it, beat 4 ounces (112g) of softened cream cheese and 1/4 cup (60g) of softened unsalted butter together on medium speed until smooth. Beat in 1 cup (120g) of confectioners sugar, 1/2 teaspoon of pure vanilla extract, and a pinch of salt until combined. Spread on cooled loaf.

- **Banana Bread Muffins:** Use this banana bread recipe to make 15 banana bread muffins. Spoon the batter into a lined or greased muffin pan (fill each to the top with batter) and bake for 5 minutes at 425°F (218°C); then, keeping the muffins in the oven, reduce the oven temperature to 350°F (177°C). Bake for an additional 16–17 minutes or until a toothpick inserted in the center comes out clean. The total bake time for the banana bread muffins is about 21–23 minutes. The initial burst of hot air helps those muffins rise nice and tall!

- **No Sour Cream** or **Yogurt?** Feel free to use 1/3 cup mashed banana (in addition to the 2 cups), unsweetened applesauce, or even canned pumpkin puree.

- **Frozen Bananas:** You can use frozen bananas here. Thaw the frozen bananas. Drain off any excess liquid, mash, then use as instructed in the recipe. Try not to mash too much or else you'll be left with 2 cups of banana-y liquid; some chunks are great.

- **Chocolate Chips:** I love this bread with chocolate chips, too. Feel free to add 1 cup of your favorite chocolate chips. No need to leave out the nuts if you add the chocolate chips. Chocolate chips and nuts are both optional.